Silver Foxes

M.R. ANGLIN

PROLOGUE

An excerpt pieced together from a corrupted copy of *Truth behind the Legends: A dictionary of your favorite myths and the scientific explanation behind them,* a digi-book found in Jelu shortly after its destruction.

Sil[ver F]oxes: n. refers to a race of Exp . . . [foxes] who . . . silver in color . . . entries in . . . and myths. Most common reference in f[airy tales], usu. . . . beautiful princess . . . a Silver Fox . . . her rescue.

The Myth: Long ago when the universe was young, the planet Clorth stood on the brink of destru[ctio]n. [The inhabitants] were found guilty of treason [against the gods] . . . [but] the wise man, Deedanus, appeased the gods by offering to them any one thing . . . desired. Flousa, the goddess of nature, chose for herself a certain flower . . . deemed worthy. Disutrine, god[dess of be]auty, reserved the right to choose any man or woman, boy [or girl] to serve . . . [in] her temple. Ham[atan, god of war], choose the iron smithies . . . weapons were made. All the gods and goddesses chose . . . except Rophim, [god of storms], king of the gods. He found nothing to appease him . . . [and vowed to] destroy Clorth . . . [if he] could not be appeased by .

. . moon rose over the mountain o[f the go]ds, a thing that happened once [a year].

[A year passed and] he found nothing to appease him . . . [As] Rophim walked through the woods on the east of the river Gordón . . . he came upon a beautiful vixen . . . [her]bs in the woods. His heart burned . . . he saw her . . . took on the form [of a] fox, and . . . wo[oed] her . . . and took her to be his bride, and . . . was appeased.

The vixen conceived . . . [and gave birth to] a son, Thrort . . . born with fur ma[de of] silver, and . . . . unable to control storms . . . [a]ble to fly, cast lightning bolts, and repel enemy attacks. He roamed the land righting wrongs and defeating monsters.

Time passed and his mother grew old. Rophim . . . [brought her] a fruit that grew on the mountain of the gods. Once eaten, this fruit would make her immortal . . . tried to get Thrort, her [son], to eat, but he refused . . . [instead chose to] marry and live among mortals. So Thrort . . . [begat] a son, [ano]ther Silve[r Fo]x.

. . . Silver Fo[xes] became numerous on Clorth. Some were noble, but far more used [their powers for evil]. Rophim saw this and cursed the line of Thrort . . . [All foxes in his] line were born gray, and only if they proved themselves . . . [regained] the powers of Thrort.

[Explan]ation: Few . . . [believe] Silver Foxes actually existed. Those that do claim . . . were nothing more than . . .

The remaining data was too corrupted and was unable to be recovered . . . much to the chagrin of the book's owner.

CHAPTER 1

The sun set on two fox kits huddled by the remains of a wall in the middle of a sea of rubble.

Broken bricks and cinder blocks, rocks, rebar, demolished signs, ruined cars, and other debris had piled up in heaps where the buildings had tossed them when they had collapsed. Clouds of smoke lingered in the air and mingled with the settling dust. Through the haze, orange rays of light filtered down and shimmered on the wasteland that used to be a city. Among it all the two foxes sat, almost motionless in the deepening gloom.

The first fox, a five-year-old kit, had gray fur gleaming in the lingering sunset. Dust covered her tattered dress, the diaper bag next to her, and her black hair. She leaned against the remains of a broken wall in order to get a better grasp on the second kit, a one year old baby with white fur. The white kit whimpered and squirmed in her sister's arms, and this soft crying caused a wolf to turn aside from his task.

The wolf went by the name of J.R. Dunsworth. He peeked around the cracked wall and stared at the two kits sitting in the ruins. When his shadow fell over the gray kit, she turned her eyes to him and gazed at his face.

J.R. blinked at this little girl. She wasn't crying; she didn't scream at the sight of him; she didn't even make a sound. Rather she studied him the same way he studied her. And as she did, she pursed her lips as if she didn't quite approve of what she saw.

J.R. glanced down at himself to see what it was about him had offended her. His shirt was relatively clean, his pants without holes, so . . . wait a minute! His ears pricked. What did he care what she thought of him? The better question was, what was she doing here alone with a baby in the middle of a demolished city? He opened his mouth to ask but closed it again. This was none of his business. The parents were probably around somewhere. He'd keep an eye out for them as he continued with his own task.

Feeling rather proud of himself for being so selfless, he turned to go on his way.

"Hey, mister." The gray kit set her sister down to stand. "My sister's been crying for a long time. She's hungry. Do you have any milk?"

J.R. glanced at her out of the corner of his eye as she stood. She smiled at him and tilted her head so her hair fell to the side, sending dust wafting into the air. Her brown eyes flashed gold when they caught the light.

Something about those eyes—so bright and devoid of fear— stabbed J.R. in the gut. He found himself stammering without realizing. "I . . . uh . . ."

"Hm . . . can you talk, mister?" The kit flattened one of her ears and screwed her mouth to the side. "Maybe you got left behind too. You can stay with us if you want."

"Huh?" J.R. shook his head to clear it. "I can talk."

"Oh. Then do you have milk?" The kit dug in the diaper bag and removed an empty canister. "I ran out." She turned to the white kit. "My sister's been crying so hard, she can't cry anymore."

J.R. looked at the baby. She wiggled on the ground, moaning and writhing. Her tiny fists clenched and unclenched and her toes curled. Must be starving. "Where are your parents, kid?"

The kit hung her head. "They went away."

J.R. clenched his teeth. What a predicament! Two helpless girls alone in the middle of a wasteland . . . not even *he* could leave them alone like this. "Yeah, kid. I'll get you some milk." He swung around, beckoned to them over his shoulder, and led them to where he had left his speeder on the side of the crippled road. At least he only had to get them milk. After they were fed, he'd find someplace to dump 'em . . . there had to be placed for missing children to go. He wouldn't have to deal with them for more than a few hours.

"Alright, Kid. Get on!" When J.R. turned to help them on the speeder . . . the kits were nowhere to be seen. "Eh?" He scanned the area for them.

He spotted the kit scrambling over the rubble, nearly bent back double with the weight of her sister and the diaper bag.

"Hold on. I'm coming." The kit raised her leg to climb over a boulder, lost her balance, and fell backward. Clutching the baby to keep her from flying over her head, the kit slid on her tail until she came to a halt on the loose stones. "You okay, Kat?" She held up her sister to examine her.

The baby blinked before giving her a toothy grin.

J.R. smacked his forehead with his palm. "No good deed goes unpunished, Dunsworth." He strode over to them, pinched the baby's scruff between his thumb and forefinger, and carried her to the speeder. The baby turned her eyes to him and gave a tiny giggle.

"Wow, mister. You're strong!" The kit trotted after him, towing the bag behind her.

J.R set the baby in the hover platform attached to his speeder— a vehicle based on an ancient two-wheeled vehicle . . . called a motorcycle, if J.R. recalled correctly.

The kit watched him set the baby on. "Where are we going?"

"We're going to get your milk." J.R. caught the kit by the scruff. "I don't have any on me." He set her beside her sister.

"Of course you don't have any *on* you. If you did, you'd be all wet." The kit cackled, almost falling backwards onto the platform.

The baby gave a more robust laugh at her sister's antics.

A smile slipped onto J.R.'s face, but he slapped it away before the kit saw it. Instead, he mounted the speeder, started the engine, and sped off down the remains of the road.

CHAPTER 2

The town of South Haston lay tucked away within the valleys
of the Drymairadian Mountains. Its inhabitants made their living
cultivating this area as a ski town in the winter, a camp site in the
summer, and a rich man's playground year round. Its green forests
and gentle slopes—sometimes rising to several hundred feet above
sea level—along with backdrops of purplish mountains stretching
into the sky, allowed visitors and residents alike to stop and breathe
whenever they wanted.

And from her perch atop a ladder, Celeste could see it all. Or
she would have if she turned her eyes to look out the windows of
the gilded Ballroom she stood in. The entire wall behind her was
made of picture windows extending floor to ceiling and
overlooking a garden flushed with yellow and red flowers and
fountains tinkling in the air. Bees buzzed around the colored
blooms, trying to get in their last pick-ups of nectar before the day
faded away. Inside, a polished marble floor reflected Celeste's
image, the golden lights of the crystal chandelier she was cleaning,
the paneled walls, and brown, floral print wallpaper. If she looked
down, she could have seen the entire scene reflected upside down
to her. On normal days, she'd be fascinated by it.

But today wasn't a normal day. Today, Celeste was too busy
trying to keep her balance to waste time looking out at the freedom
displayed outdoors or at the glory showcased indoors. Usually,

balance wasn't an issue; she could do her tasks with her eyes closed. But today, she couldn't move an inch without her stomach churning and rumbling and sloshing and heaving. It felt like she was on a perpetual rollercoaster, her stomach leaping in her abdomen.

She swallowed hard and clutched the top of the ladder for balance. Her mouth watered freely. She felt like she was going to—

"There she is!" The golden doors burst open, and Terrance Claybourne strode in with open arms.

Celeste started, almost falling off the ladder and making her stomach flip. Her master, Terrance Claybourne, was an orange tabby dressed in a dark blue suit with no tie. His tail twitched as he walked, and his smile widened—showing off his sharp teeth. Celeste's chest tightened. She couldn't tell if he was seething or happy. But there wasn't much difference between his emotions— he could punish her equally hard whether he was in a good mood or bad. And if he had come looking for her then . . . oh, no! She bit her bottom lip. She should have been on to weeding the back gardens by now. What would he do to her for running behind schedule? Lock her in a closet? Beat her? Or worse . . . She pulled at the collar around her neck . . . shock-discipline?

"There's the pride of my collection working as hard as can be!" Terrance's smile widened, revealing his fangs. "Come down here, Celeste. Let my guest have a look at you."

For the first time, Celeste noted a forest cat trailing Terrance. He was quite a bit younger than Terrance and had a bright smile. She climbed down the ladder, slowly. Every step seemed to set her stomach off-kilter.

"Wow." The cat circled Celeste as soon as she stepped onto the ground. "I've never seen a gray-furred fox before."

"To be clear, she's a red fox with a gray color mutation." Terrance raised his chin with a triumphant chuckle. "Quite rare."

Celeste's stomach heaved. "Mr. Claybourne. I—"

"Quiet, Celeste. I'm busy."

"Her fur is so silky." The forest cat ran his hands over her fur. Celeste held out her arms and let him do it. She was used to this sort of treatment. It was the reason Terrance dressed her as he did: in a mini-skirt and a white halter which left her stomach exposed— all to show off as much of her fur as possible.

"Incredible," the newcomer said. "And her hair—it's so shiny and black, it's almost bluish!"

"We call her particular hair color 'raven.'" Terrance grinned as if he had created her himself.

The stranger stroked his chin. "How much do you want for her?"

"She is not for sale." Terrance chuckled. "I showed her to you so you can get an idea of what to aspire to when you start your own collection in earnest."

Celeste's stomach tightened. Her bottom of her mouth—where her saliva glands rested—tingled. "Mr. Claybourne—"

"Shut up, Celeste."

"But I don't feel so—hurk!" Celeste slapped her hand over her mouth.

Terrance whirled on her, his ears flat and his teeth bared. "Celeste, I said—eh?"

Celeste couldn't hold it anymore. Her stomach heaved, and its contents exploded from her mouth. And splashed right at Terrance's feet.

"Ugh!" Terrance's guest hopped back.

Terrance stood motionless a moment, his ears flattening.

"Mr. Claybourne . . ." Celeste said between groans. "I—"

"My shoes," Terrance said barely above a whisper. He snarled and raised his orange eyes to meet hers. "You wench!" He smacked her across the cheek, raking his extended claws against the side of her face.

The momentum sent Celeste flying. She collapsed on the floor. Four deep gashes burned her cheek. Trembling, she scrambled away from him. But he wasn't done with her yet. Something worse would be coming, and . . .

"Hurk!" Her impending punishment fled from her mind as her stomach flopped again. She got to her hands and knees and heaved.

"Ew!" The other cat stepped away from the mess she had made. "Does this happen often?"

"Not as much as you would think." Terrance kicked the filth off his shoes right in Celeste's face.

The cat examined Celeste. "She looks like she's going to throw up again. What do you do when they get sick?"

"When you have as large a collection as mine, you need an in-house clinic. No use spending money on them if they die on you a few years after." Terrance swung around to the door, beckoning over his shoulder with a finger. "Come on. I'll show you." He pushed open the door with more force than was necessary. "You, there," he said to another one of his collection outside the door. "Go in there and clean up that mess."

"I guess I have to carry her." The other cat hefted Celeste. Her stomach hopped, and she held her hands over her mouth again. "I swear, if she gets any on me," the cat muttered, "Terrance is going to have to pay for a drycleaner." He snorted through his nose and jogged through the door, jostling Celeste as he went.

* * *

"Now I know I had another bottle of emetic around here somewhere." Isha Doran, the resident doctor for Terrance Claybourne's collection, examined the medicine cabinet inside the estate's clinic. The place was sterile in all senses of the word. Sterile décor—all white, with no decorations . . . just the stainless steel medical equipment housed in their proper steel cabinets, a stainless steel desk with a computer on it, and a line of beds against the wall with crisp, white sheets; sterile air—smelling of disinfectant and so cold it made Isha's fur fluff out; and every surface sterilized—no germs in her clinic, ever.

The steel medicine cabinet Isha stared at was nothing more than a set of shelves stretching from floor to ceiling with vials of medicines and bandages packed within. The entire thing was enclosed by locked, glass doors to which Isha had the only key . . . a key she kept chained to the lapel of her lab coat with a retractable keychain.

"How in the world could I have misplaced an entire bottle of medicine?" Isha held up her inventory list again, and then counted the bottles on the third shelf. Sure enough, one short. "I'd better find out what happened to it before Terrance uses it as an excuse to get me into his collection." She shuddered at the thought.

"Here we are!" The door to the clinic burst open, and Terrance waltzed in. "Welcome to my clinic, FC." He held the door open. "I spare no expense to keep my collection healthy. In fact, I'm thinking of expanding this wing."

"Great . . . but where can I put her?" A forest cat ambled in, holding Celeste in her hands. The poor vixen had her head lolled to the side, and her tongue hanging out of her mouth. Her face had taken on greenish hues.

"Oh, dear! Celeste!" Isha rushed over to put a hand on Celeste's forehead. Her skin was clammy to the touch, and her eyes glazed over. "What happened to you?"

"I don't feel good." Celeste clamped her mouth shut as she retched.

"I think she ate something bad," the cat known as FC struggled to get a better grip on her. "Started blowing chunks all over the place."

Terrance narrowed his eyes. "I think she is faking it."

"Tell it to your shoes." FC motioned to Terrance's feet. Isha glanced at them. A wet spot with white splotches had appeared on his expensive, leather shoes.

"Set her down on the bed there." Isha motioned to one of the beds, while pulling a penlight from her lab coat pocket.

"My stomach hurts," wailed Celeste weakly as FC set her down.

"Oh, dear." Isha opened Celeste's eyes to shine her light in them. "This doesn't look good at all."

"Oooo. A red panda." FC, freed of his burden of carrying Celeste, circled Isha, examining her from head to toe. "Is she one of your collection too, Terrance?"

Isha narrowed her eyes at him. "Back off, twerp."

FC's eyes widened. He stepped back some.

"I wish Isha was part of my collection. But Dr. Doran is too smart to put herself in debt. I'll have to settle for paying for her presence here." Terrance purred in an unsettling way. "But if I had a chance, I'd snap her up at once. Ooo, the thought of it makes me shiver in anticipation."

Isha stifled a shudder.

"She's getting up in years, though, don't you think?" FC stroked his chin. "Ears starting to droop; glasses; gray strands among her red fur. She'd be a lot older than the rest of your collection."

"True, I do like to buy specimens in their prime—teens to late twenties— but I would make an exception for her." Terrance raised his chin as a father who was about to give some good advice to a son. "You see, red pandas are rare in this country, and there isn't much chance I'd see one in their prime without smuggling him in, and I have yet to find a reliable trafficking source. Sometimes, you have to take what you can get when building your collection.

Remember that, FC."

"Yes, sir." FC gave a mock salute.

Isha's fur rose along her neck. The way Terrance spoke about people sent disgust rushing up her spine in waves. But she had a salary to earn and bills to pay. If she wanted to stay out of his collection herself, she had to continue on. So she turned her mind off of Terrance's disgusting conversation and focused her attention to Celeste.

"What the—" Isha turned Celeste's cheek to the light. "*Some*one gave her some gashes across her face." She shot a glare at Terrance.

Terrance shrugged. "She ruined my shoes."

"I would think you'd be gentler with her since she's the so-called 'Pride of your Collection.'"

"And she is." Terrance's ears lay flat. "But no one disrespects me."

Celeste rolled over on her side. Her face contorted with agony.

"It's not like she could help it." Isha muttered but said nothing out loud. Instead she picked up a medical scanner. "Let's see what else is wrong with you, Celeste. Hold st—oh!" She sighed. "Terrance, please remove the shock collar."

"No."

Isha rolled her eyes. "Must we go through this every time?"

"Why do you need to take it off?" FC crossed his arms. "It's supposed to keep them contained, isn't it?"

"As I've told Terrance several times, the collar interferes with the scanner." Isha shot FC a look warning him to mind his own business. FC raised his hands and clamped his mouth shut. Isha turned her attention to Terrance. "I can't make an accurate diagnosis with it on, and you know that, Terrance."

"What do I care?" Terrance snorted in Celeste's direction, his whiskers stiffening. "This one has tried to escape five times last month. She will not have an attempt at a sixth."

Isha sighed through her nose. Sometimes dealing with his man wasn't worth her salary. "Seeing as though abdominal pain and nausea can be symptoms of anything ranging from food poisoning to the stomach flu to appendicitis—which can be fatal, by the way—I would think you'd want me to diagnose her properly. Now, take off the collar!"

Terrance turned up his nose and narrowed his eyes. His gaze shifted to Celeste who whimpered on the bed as she held her stomach. He sniffed. "Fine! But first!" He stooped to the ground and pulled out a chain attached to the bed. "Had this installed since the last time you've been in here, Celeste." He attached the chain to her foot. "We will not try anything this time, will we, Celeste?" He stroked her hair.

Celeste whined and shook her head.

"Good answer." Terrance removed the collar from around her neck.

"Thank you," Isha said. "Now, shoo. Out!"

"What? Why?" FC said. "I want to see."

"Because Terrance's presence in my clinic causes my patients' heartrate and blood pressure to skyrocket." Isha snorted at FC. "And I don't like you. Now, out. Both of you."

"Her attitude sucks," FC muttered as he walked out.

"I'll be back in the morning to check on her, Isha." Terrance pointed at Celeste, his nails extended and catching the light. "And if I find you have faked this, Celeste, you will be sorry."

"Out!" Isha shoved him out and slammed the door in their faces. "Well, he's gone."

"Thank you," Celeste said barely above a whisper.

"No problem, sweetie." Isha picked up her scanner to examine Celeste.

The scanner was a flat machine with a screen on one side. It was the latest model, but the results that showed up on the screen were undecipherable. Even with her years of schooling and decades of medical experience, Isha had to turn to a computer to translate the results . . . which is what she did now.

"Oh! Look at that," she said when the results displayed on screen. "Hm, mystery solved." She sighed. "I should have never let you help me in the clinic last week." She looked at Celeste over her glasses. "You're the one who took the medicine from the medicine cabinet, aren't you?"

Celeste's ears flicked down. Then she ducked her face into her chest and nodded. Her tail slipped between her legs. "I'm sorry." She retched, covering her mouth with her hands.

"I've heard stories of slaves who try to overdose on medicine as a way to escape the horrors of slavery, but in addition to trying to abuse a restricted substance, you made another bad choice, sweetie." Isha stroked Celeste's hair out of her face. "The medicine you swiped is an emetic. It induces vomiting. You didn't take enough to be life-threatening, but you will be throwing up all night."

Celeste opened her mouth to respond, but instead of words she threw up all over the bed and floor. "Ugh!" she groaned and flopped all over the mess.

"I can't have you doing *that* all night. I won't have a moment's rest if I'm cleaning up after you." Isha glanced at the door. "I know what Terrance said, but you're in no condition to go anywhere except to the bathroom." She pulled a key from her retractable keyring attached to her lab coat and unlocked Celeste's leg.

As soon as she was free, Celeste bolted to the bathroom.

Isha stood at the bathroom door. "That will probably be your view for most of the night. There's nothing I can give you to help your nausea. You have to bear through it." She turned to the mess on the bed and floor. "I'll clean up and continue with my inventory. I'll have to lock you in tonight, but my room is behind that door on the other side of the clinic. So I'll be with you all night long. You can call if you need anything, and I—" She turned back to Celeste and halted.

Celeste looked up at her with eyes half closed. "And you'll what?" Her words slurred together.

Isha examined Celeste a moment. "And . . . I'll come right out."

"Thank you." Celeste rested her hand on her arm. "You're so kind." She retched again and thrust her face in the toilet. She vomited.

"Right." Isha turned away from her. She glanced at Celeste over her shoulder as she went to the closet to get new bed clothes. Now, she wasn't sure, but she could have sworn she had seen Celeste smiling—a triumphant, victorious smile. But, no. That was nonsense. Celeste was a slave who had managed to get herself sick on vomit-inducing medicine—medicine Terrance would exact retribution for stealing. She had everything against her, and nothing to look forward to? What could she possibly have to smile about?

CHAPTER 3

Five hours. It took five hours to drive from Jelu to Justin's Ridge. Far too long for a starving baby. But there was no place closer where J.R. could stop. Happily, the baby fell asleep pretty early in the trip. But not the kid. She kept blabbering and blathering for four hours straight as the sun set and the moon rose.

"And my *Mamai* said we're not allowed to talk to strangers, but you're okay because my friend told us you were coming to take care of us. But anyway, you know what she did? She talked to a guy she didn't know on the street. And I said, '*Mamai*, we're not supposed to talk to strangers.' And she said—"

But the time he pulled up to a grocery store in a line of shops, J.R. was ready to pull his fur out. He unmounted the speeder without even turning off the engine.

"... and that's why I hate the purple pony in the show." The Kid shut up long enough to survey the wood paneled buildings with the faded, weather-stained, red awning. "Where are we?"

"A store." J.R. turned his back to her, hoping she'd get the hint to shut up. "Gotta find a way to get rid o' her," he muttered. "Maybe leave her on a stoop somewhere."

"Here, mister." The Kid set her sister aside to climb out of the speeder. The motion caused the baby to wake up and whimper, gearing up for a wail. "This is the kind of milk you have to get." She held out a yellow canister to J.R. "*Mamai* says the other kinds upsets Kat's tummy."

Mamai? J.R. scratched his hair. She had been saying that a lot.

She must mean "Mommy." Weird accent the kid had. "Is that right?" He snatched the can from her.

"And they make her poop stink."

"Thanks for the thought." J.R. barged into the store leaving the kit behind. A bell tinkled as he walked in.

The store was built with dark wood, and that, along with an awning shutting out most of the light, made the store look darker than it was under the pale moonlight. Barrels of pickles and apples and pyramids of canned foods stood at the head of each aisle. A ceiling fan twirled above, but it moved so slowly J.R. felt it was more for effect than to cool the place down. A store, alright. But an old one. The place hadn't changed since he was a teenager. All part of its charm.

"Who's there?" A brown dog with floppy ears and dark brown hair that fell down her back stepped out of an aisle. She had a broom in her hands and wore a full green apron. "I thought I'd locked up."

"Glad you didn't."

"Wasn't expecting you back till mornin'." Melody leaned on her broom. "Couldn't find anyone to shack up with for the night?"

"Had a minor emergency." J.R. leaned out of the aisle to grin at her. "But I'd be happy to shack up with you if you're offering."

"I'll pass, thanks." Melody balked as she returned to her sweeping. "I'd like to respect myself in the morning."

"Your loss." J.R. shrugged as he wandered down the aisle again. "How's the old man?"

"Sleepin'."

"Wasn't feeling well last I heard."

"He's fine now."

"Good." J.R. returned to his hunt. He'd grown up in this town so he knew this store like the back of his hand—or nearly. He had a firm command of the alcohol, chips, and meat section, learned enough about the produce section to know how to avoid it, and could guess approximately where the milk, cheese, and frozen food section was. But the baby section . . .

"This is like a labyrinth." J.R. glanced down aisle after aisle until . . . yes, right next to the feminine products. He cringed. Another section he'd never be caught dead in.

"This is obscene." He kept his eyes straight forward as he passed various "napkins" that didn't look like any napkins he'd ever seen, liners, and sport versions of woman's unmentionables. He never would have thought it, but he was relieved when he found himself among the diapers and formula.

"Let's see . . ." J.R. studied the empty canister the Kid had given him.

"Rexwim Formula: Vulpine Mix. As gentle as mother's milk," had been printed beneath a picture of a red vixen holding a fox kit to her chest. At first he couldn't imagine why they would have a child pressed against her like that. It looked like the kit would suffocate. And then why was one of her sleeves off her shoulder. Pretty strange picture to put on a can of . . . oh!

J.R. balked. "I'll never look at them the same way again." He glanced at the shelves for a match to the canister. There were several Rexwim Formulas in various colors, each meant for separate species. The yellow one caught his eye. Yup . . . he compared it to his own. A perfect match. But, wait. Blue lettering was printed on the bottom, "Just mix with water."

Water? He shook the canister. Ah, it's a powder. He sighed and went to grab a bottle of water from the refrigerator.

"Hey, J.R.? Almost done?" Melody called from the front of the store. "I'd like to lock up soon."

"Yeah. I—" J.R. halted. He glanced at the canister then toward Melody's voice. He couldn't let her see this. If she did, she'd know he'd gone soft and brought two kits home. The story would run all over town—possibly the world. It'd ruin his street-cred. No one would ever respect him again. Worse, Melody would never let him live it down.

He slipped the canister into his coat and headed to the door. "Since you want to lock up, I'll go ahead and leave."

"Hold it!" Melody pointed as she stepped into the aisle. "Don't you dare go out without paying."

Drat! J.R. turned. "Uh . . . Look, Mel . . . I can explain . . ."

"Explain what? I don't care if it is water, you're not getting away with anything from this store. You get away with too much already." Melody held out her hand. "$1.79, please."

"Oh, right." J.R. dug into his pocket while trying to keep his coat closed and the canister hidden from view. He withdrew a bill and handed it to her. "Keep the change."

"Keep the change?" Melody angled one of her ears back. "Why are you being so generous all of a sudden? And since when do you drink water?"

"Just . . . just thirsty." He backed out the door. "Okay, bye." He darted out. And nearly tripped over the Kid. "What are you doing, Kid?" He glanced over his shoulder at Melody. She merely shook her head and headed back to her business . . . forgetting to lock the door. Again.

The Kid pointed. "Your picture's on the wall."

"Huh?" J.R. turned to where she pointed. A reward poster had been tacked up near one of the store windows. His mouth curled into a smirk at the picture of himself, and he glanced at the list of offenses he had committed: Grand Theft, Larceny, Murder, Impersonating the Royal Plumber . . . he chuckled when he remembered that job. And the reward: one and a half million dollars. "Hey, I broke a broke a million!"

"Wan . . . ted." The Kid cocked her head as she sounded out the word. "Wanted? What's that mean?"

"Uh . . . um . . ." J.R. scratched his whiskers. How to explain to a Kid he was a wanted criminal—a Master Thief? While he never cared much about others' opinion, somehow he couldn't stomach the thought of wrecking this kid's innocence. Must mean he had a decent streak in him. He'd have to get rid of it after he figured out how to get rid of these kits. "Uh, it means a lot of people wanted to hang out with me. Yeah . . . I'm wanted for parties and stuff."

The Kid's eyes widened. "So you're like a clown?" She clapped her hands and bobbed up and down. "Do something funny."

"Ain't the baby hungry?" J.R. shuffled her toward the speeder. "Here. Take the milk."

"Oh, thanks." After taking the canister, she climbed up on the platform, and rummaged through the diaper bag for a baby bottle. The minute the baby saw the bottle, she wiggled and clawed at the Kid's hand.

"Wait a minute, Kathra." The kit held the bottle out of the baby's grasp. "Let me fix it."

The baby—Kathra, J.R. gathered—glared at her sister. She gave an angry yell and pouted, her face turning red. But she did stop clawing at her sister.

The Kid opened the canister, fished around in the powder until she found a small, plastic scoop, and shoveled two of them into the bottle. "Where's the water?"

J.R. held it up, proud of his foresight. "Here." He opened it and handed it to her.

Her tongue sticking out of her mouth a bit, the Kid poured the water onto the powder with the expert hand of someone who'd practiced the motion a lot.

J.R. scrunched up his muzzle. At her age, he could barely pour orange juice in a glass, much less pour water into a baby bottle. How long had they been on their own?

"Kat, stop! Let me mix it!"

The yelling jerked J.R. back to the present. The Kid, once again held the bottle away from the baby, who clawed at her hand to get it.

"Wait!" The Kid went to give the bottle a shake. The top flew off and half-mixed formula splashed in J.R.'s face.

"Oops." She looked up at him. "Sorry. The top wasn't on right."

The baby halted in her tracks. She held her hands together and looked up at him with large bluish-green eyes . . . the epitome of an apologetic angel.

J.R. wiped formula out of his eyes, snatched the bottle from the kid, and poured more water in. He screwed the top on properly and gave it a good shake before thrusting it back into the Kid's hands.

"Thank you." The Kid handed the bottle to the baby who snatched the bottle and chugged it so fast it looked as if she would choke herself.

"Whoa!" J.R.'s eyes widened as he watched her drain the bottle. "She's gonna suck the bottle in."

The Kid nodded gravely. "She didn't eat since last night."

Wait . . . J.R. stared at her out of the corner of his eye. If the baby hadn't eaten, then . . . "What about you, Kid? When was the last time you ate?"

"Umm . . ." She raised her eyes to the dark sky. "Yesterday morning."

"Then you'll want something to eat, too."

She smiled and nodded.

"But where am I gonna find something for the Kid? Everything closes up early 'round here." J.R. scratched his cheek. "Ah, yeah. There's the new fast food joint. Maybe they're still open. You like burgers, Kid?"

The Kid pouted. "My name's Xena. Don't call me 'Kid'

anymore."

"Yeah?" J.R. thrust his chin toward the baby who had fallen on her back while chugging. "And her name?"

"She's Kathra."

"Thought so. You call me J.R." He mounted the speeder. "I've never been a 'mister' before."

Xena settled into a corner of the platform. "My *Mamai* says it's not nice to call grownups by their first name."

J.R.'s ears angled back. He hated being lectured—even by a five-year-old. "Do you see your mommy 'round here?"

"No, my *Mamai* went away." She drew up her knees. "She and Daddy left us with Auntie Rose because bad people were coming after *Mamai*. Then Auntie Rose said it wasn't safe at her house and took us to her friend's house. Then *they* left us with *their* friend. They didn't want us anymore so they took us to their friend's house, and . . ." She paused and counted on her fingers. "Then the ground shook and all the buildings fell down."

"So you were in the city when it collapsed?"

Xena nodded, her eyes shiny and moist. "And it's all my fault. *Mamai* and Daddy left us because I wasn't a good girl." She drew up her knees and buried her face in them. Her shoulders shook.

J.R.'s ears fell back. Crying? He didn't know how to handle a crying kid. "H-hey . . . Kid. S-Stop. D-don't cry. You're not a baby, right?"

"I'm not crying. I'm not a crybaby!" Xena glared at him with such fury that J.R. flinched. Quite a contrast to the tears flowing down her cheeks. Kathra put down her bottle long enough to pat Xena's arms.

"Ouggle?" Kathra looked up at her with tears in her eyes.

"I don't cry anymore." Xena wiped her eyes with her arm. "If I cry, Kat starts crying too."

"Good." J.R. gave her a grin. "'Cause I hate crybabies."

Xena studied his face for a moment before cracking a smile.

"So." He started his speeder. "You like burgers, Kid?"

"I said don't call me Kid!"

"I'll call you what I want." J.R. took off down the road. "After all, what are you going to do about it?"

CHAPTER 4

The rolling hills of South Haston snuggled in deep shadow, the moon glinting off chateaus and gleaming off the trees and grass on the hilltops. In Terrance Claybourne's clinic, moonlight sent long shadows stretching across the cold, tile floor and glistened off of Isha's medical equipment.

But Celeste didn't see any of it. All night, her view had been the inside of the toilet bowl. The stench from her regurgitated meals made her want to heave again. She wanted to stand up, but she couldn't. She was being held captive by her wavering stomach. By now her abdomen was empty, but it didn't stop her body from trying to evacuate her insides. Celeste swallowed hard and turned to the clock on the wall. 2:30 am.

Celeste pushed herself to her feet even as her stomach protested. "Come on, Celeste. Pull it together." She swallowed the spit often preceding a retch. "You didn't risk stealing the emetic, betraying Isha's trust, risking Terrance's rage, and spending the night with your face in a toilet to let this chance slip by. Go! Even if you make a mess on your way out." She pushed herself to her feet and stumbled into the clinic. Bracing herself on the bathroom door's frame, she scanned the room for Isha's computer. It was sitting on the desk where Isha had left it after she had scanned Celeste. Lucky break.

"Maybe she thought I was too sick to do anything with it." Celeste stumbled over to the computer. "Or too dumb." Most of the slaves she knew could neither read nor write, but Celeste was a special case. Though she had been sold into slavery as a child, she had learned to read and write when she was a girl. Reading had been one of her favorite things. Not that it mattered now.

She paused as another wave of nausea slammed into her before pushing the power button.

A login screen appeared.

Celeste bit her lips together. "Sorry, Isha. You've been so nice to me, but . . ." She tapped in Isha's password one letter at a time. ". . . but never type in your password where prying eyes can see."

The screen changed to Isha's normal desktop. She had a picture of her, her children, and her grandchildren in the background. They seemed like such nice people. Celeste opened a program to get rid of it.

"Oh please, oh please, oh please!" Celeste closed her eyes to pray to whatever deity would hear her. "Please let this computer be connected to Terrance's slave database." She took a deep breath and clicked on the search icon. It took a while to find the right search parameters—Celeste only had a first grade reading and spelling level, after all—but finally, "The Claybourne Collection" appeared on the screen.

"This is it!" Celeste slapped her hands over her mouth. She had to keep it quiet. Such an outburst could wake everyone. She glanced one way then another. The clinic was still shrouded in silence—only the ticking clock made any noise. Celeste watched it for a moment—strange that Isha liked those old mechanical clocks when everyone else had moved on to digital centuries ago. Still, it was Isha's charm. She held on to things like old clocks and common decency. It was why Celeste had been able to manipulate her so.

She turned her mind away from those thoughts and looked at the screen. There was her profile—all the information Terrance had on her including her ownership papers and her list price—the price she or someone on her behalf had to pay to buy her freedom. She glanced around before removing a crumpled piece of paper from her bra—an ad she had seen in a copy of Terrance's *Collector's Monthly* magazine. Underneath a picture of four well-dressed business people, the copy read:

> Are you an owner looking to liquidate your collection?
>
> A loved one looking to free your special

someone but don't have the cash?

A slave willing to work for your freedom?

The GFG Corporation has the answer. As part of our Freedom-Work Initiative, "The Freedom Project,"* we buy slaves for full list price in exchange for participating in our Debt-Worker Experience Program. After working for us for a predetermined length of time, the debt is repaid, and your slave is free! It's that easy!

Call for a free consultation or visit us at one of our participating office locations.

*Slave papers and list price required. We will do our best to work with you to retrieve them.

Celeste would never have seen the ad if Terrance hadn't been so furious as to shred the magazine with his bare claws.

"How dare they advertise in *my* magazine?" he had shrieked.

So of course, Celeste had to investigate. Seeing the ad was the greatest day of her life. After some research, Celeste had found the closest office location was in a place called Jelu. Jelu—the place of her freedom.

"Let's see . . . my papers are here . . . print . . . and . . . hey! What *is* my list price? . . . oh!" Celeste eyes widened as she saw the price Terrance had listed for her freedom. "$654,785?" She flopped back in her chair as her stomach dropped. "No one's ever going to pay that much for me!" But she still had to try. She couldn't give up her only chance at freedom.

She collected her papers from the printer, darted to the clinic door, and yanked on it. Locked.

Celeste bit her bottom lip. Isha did say she had to lock her in to keep her from escaping.

Isha's bedroom—there for the days she had to stay on call for some reason and couldn't go home—was on the other side of the clinic. Celeste peeked in. The room was shrouded in darkness with only a sliver of moon and streetlights peeking in through the drawn curtains to illuminate it. Celeste could barely make out Isha's form sleeping on the bed. She slipped in and glanced around. Isha had keys on her lab coat, so perhaps they were still there. But where was her lab coat? She spotted it hanging on a peg behind the door.

As silently as she could, Celeste unclipped the keys from the lab coat's lapel. They jingled as she moved them, but Isha kept right on sleeping. Celeste paused, said a silent apology to the doctor who had been so nice to her, and tip-toed out. Unlocking the clinic door, she eased it open.

"I hope you don't get in too much trouble because of me, Isha." Celeste tip-toed out of the clinic and into the hallway.

Phase one of her escape was complete.

CHAPTER 5

The ride to J.R.'s house on the outskirts of town was quieter than the ride to Justin's Ridge. Amazing what shoving a chicken nugget kid's meal in a little girl's pie hole could accomplish. The sweet roar of his speeder's souped up engine was only interrupted by the occasional, "Want a fry, Kat?" or "No, Kat! You're too small for nuggets."

But by the time J.R. pulled up to his wooden, cabin style house in the middle of the forest west of Justin's Ridge, the food was gone and the distraction over. Xena was back to her chatty self.

"Is this where you live?" Xena said as J.R. set her on the ground. A smile spread across her face. "It's beautiful! It looks like the house in the woods in the fairy tale book *Mamai* reads to me. But, wait—" She halted, her fur standing on end. "Y-you're not a b-big, b-bad wolf, are you?"

"What?" J.R. gave a sneer exposing his sharp fangs. "What kinda fairy tales are you readin', Kid?"

"Daddy did say the book was a pile of speciest nonsense." Xena skipped to the front door. "I don't know what that means, though."

"I'm not even going to try to understand." J.R. went to pick up the baby but paused when he saw her face. Her cheeks puffed out, and a pink hue spread had spread over them. She clenched her fists with so much effort, her tail trembled. "You better not be gettin' sick." He picked her up to look in her eyes. "I don't do sick babies."

Kathra stopped to pant a few times before straining again.

J.R. sighed. He made his way to the front door and let Xena inside before walking in himself.

"Wow!" Xena's wide eyes fell over everything. "It's like a cave!"

J.R. glanced at the décor. He'd never paid much attention to the place before, but he could see why she thought "cave." Most everything was made of wood which darkened everything. The entry herded all guest to the right where the house opened up to a hallway. Right now, all of it was shrouded in darkness. He flipped on a light.

"Ooo! It looks like a tumbleweed!" Xena pointed up at the light fixture hanging in the entryway. "Oh, I know! This is not a cave. It's a . . . a . . . um . . . a salon!"

J.R.'s ears pricked. "Now, wait a minute, Kid! I don't live in no girly salon!"

"Yeah, you do! You're like a cowboy!" She galloped around as if she were riding on one of those calborros—a riding animal people used to use before cars were invented.

"Oh, a *saloon*." J.R. fingered his chin whiskers as he looked around the house. With the wood paneling on the walls, the bare wood beams on the ceiling, and all his wooden furniture, the place did have an old, rustic look to it. Yeah, he could see saloon.

"I like this house." Xena nodded her head as she put her hands on her hips—almost as if she was approving of it.

"Nice, Kid, but don't get attached. You're not—" An odor, like rotten meat cooked in sour milk wafted past J.R. nose. "Guh! What is that stench?" He pinched his nose and glanced around. Nothing unusual. He even looked under his shoes. "Did you step in something, Kid?"

"Uh, oh!" Xena pointed at Kathra. "I think she made a stinky."

"Eh?" J.R. held the baby at arm's length. Relief and satisfaction washed over her face. He took a tentative sniff. And retched. "Oh, that's foul!" He held her as far away from his nose as possible.

"She needs a diaper change." Xena stood with her hand behind her back.

Silence fell. She and J.R. stared at each other a few moments.

"So," J.R. said.

"So what?" Xena said.

"Let's get goin'. Where're the diapers?"

"I don't have any more."

J.R.'s ears angled back. "Then how are we supposed to change her?"

"Don't you have any diapers in the house?"

"I don't got kids."

"Then didn't you get any at the store?"

J.R.'s tail started to twitch. "How was I supposed to know we needed diapers?"

"Because you're the adult! Duh! The adult is supposed to know."

J.R. growled deep in his throat. "Fine!" He set the baby on the floor. "Stay here. I'll go get them." He swung open the door.

Xena rushed after him. "But, Mr. J.R.—"

"Stay there!" J.R. slammed the door in her face. "I have got to find a place to dump them." He marched to his speeder. "They're staying one night. One night, and that's all!" With a determined nod, he got on his speeder and drove through the woods back to Justin's Ridge.

***

"But, Mr. J.R.—" Xena rushed after him but halted when the door slammed in her face. She heard J.R. get on his speeder and drive away. "But . . ." She turned to Kathra. "I don't think you're supposed to leave two kids all alone by themselves."

Kathra shoved her fist in her mouth, falling on her back in the process.

"He's not a very good adult, is he, Kat?" Xena put her hands on her hips.

Kathra took her hand out of her mouth long enough to say, "A pap pag."

"Come on, Kat. Don't flop. You can sit up." Xena pulled Kathra up to her feet. "You want to try to walk?"

"Wak! Wak!" Kathra cackled at Xena. Her stench drifted up to Xena.

"Ew, Kat!" Xena let go of Kathra so fast, Kathra fell on her tail. "You really stink!"

Kathra only clapped her hands and laughed.

CHAPTER 6

"Hang on! Hang on!" Melody slipped her robe over her night clothes as she ran down the stairs leading from the apartment above the grocery store. The place always looked eerie at night—as if things hid in the shadows, waiting to jump out at her. She snarled even as a shiver went up her tail. J.R. had put those silly stories in her head as a pup, and all these years later she hadn't forgotten them.

Someone banged on the store's door—hard enough to break the glass.

"Hang on, I said!" Melody tied her robe before swinging open the door. "J.R.?" She blinked at his massive frame silhouetted against the moonlight. His sharp ears were flat, and his eyes narrowed. "What are you doing here?"

"Don't ask." J.R. pushed past her.

"Um, hello? We're closed!"

J.R. murmured something as he scanned the shelves.

Melody blew her hair out of her face. "Honestly! I was in bed, J.R.! Don't you have a shred of—"

"Melody, everythin' alright?" came a voice from upstairs—a shaky, frail sounding one.

"Yeah, Dad!" Melody paused to swallow the lump that rose in her throat when she heard his voice quivering so. "It's just J.R. Go back to sleep."

"Then tell 'em to pipe down, would ya." Her father's voice strengthened as he spoke about J.R. "I'm tryin' to sleep."

"As if he listens to me." Melody crossed her arms, but inside she smiled. Her father never could stand to look or sound weak in front of J.R. Her father, known to all as Mr. Withers, was the only source of real discipline J.R. had ever had, and he took it upon himself to always be an unshakable pillar J.R. could never break.

"Ah, hah! Here we go!" J.R. snatched a large cube off the shelf. Pasting a grin on his face, he shouted, "Pipe down yourself, old man, I'm leavin'!"

"Boy, you better run 'fore I come down there and tan your hide!" Mr. Withers shouted, his voice even stronger than before.

Melody rolled her eyes. Those two always went at it like that. She glanced the package in J.R.'s hands. "Diapers?"

J.R.'s grin disappeared. "Don't ask."

"And you better pay for whatever you took, J.R.!" Mr. Withers shouted. "Or I'll take you over my knee. You ain't too old."

"Yeah, yeah. I got it." J.R. smacked a bill on the counter. "Later, Mel." He marched out.

"Wait a minute, J.R." Melody caught the door before it closed behind him. "What are you doing with diap—"

"I said, don't ask!" J.R. drove off without another word.

Melody stood in the doorway and watched the exhaust from his speeder dissipate into the streetlight's shimmer.

"What was that all about?" She let her ears angle back. "Why would J.R. need diapers?" She chuckled to herself. "Maybe one of his girlfriends finally trapped him into taking responsibility." She tapped her elbow. It might be the most logical of explanations, but it didn't seem right. J.R. would do anything to escape responsibility. No, it wasn't likely he'd be taking care of a baby. So what were the diapers for? Well, whatever he was up to, one thing was certain: if he needed diapers, he'd probably need wipes. Which meant he'd be back in a few moments to wake her and her father up again . . . or . . . She groaned. Or she'd have to go give him the wipes. Either way, the result was the same.

"I'm not going to sleep anytime soon, am I?" Melody sighed as she walked back into the store. "Stupid J.R.!"

CHAPTER 7

"Stupid kids," J.R. muttered as he pulled up to his house for the second time that night. "Made me go all the way to the store for diapers. Diapers!" He snarled as he stomped to the front door. "If Melody says anything about this to anyone, I'll have to conveniently forget she's a girl." He flung the door open. "Shoulda gotten beer."

"Good girl, Kathra! You're walking so good!" Xena's voice rose above Kathra's laughter. J.R. turned up his nose as he closed the door. When she wasn't whining for food, the baby was always laughing. "Oh, wait! Don't touch, Kathra," came Xena's voice. "You're going to break it!"

Break it? J.R. rushed past the stairs, the kitchen, and into the TV room at the back of the house next to the dining room. He found the two standing in front of a set of wooden shelving to the right of the entertainment center. Kathra had a wooden statue in her hands, and Xena was trying to pull it from her grasp.

"Give it!" Xena said. "You'll get us in trouble!"

"Mine!" said Kathra in the most furious baby voice J.R. had ever heard.

"Kathra!" Xena yanked as hard as she could. Kathra lost hold of the statue and fell on her back while Xena fell onto her tail. The statue flew out of her hands and crashed onto the floor. It splintered into two. "Oh, no!" She covered her mouth.

J.R.'s fur settled. He didn't care about the statue. He didn't even know why he had it . . . the creepy thing. It belonged to his parents or something. But even though he didn't care about it, it didn't mean he wouldn't yell. The opportunity to scare the pants off that sassy kid was too good to pass up.

"Whaddaya think you're doin'?" J.R. shouted in his deepest, most booming voice.

Xena swung around, her eyes wide as dinner plates. "Um . . . um . . . that . . . that thing falled . . . by itself. We didn't do it!"

A lie? J.R. felt the fur on his tail stand on end. He wasn't a stranger to lies, but it irked him that she would try it with him. He marched up to her, his whiskers stiffening. "You lyin' to me, Kid?"

Xena's tail slipped between her legs. Slowly, she nodded and a whimper of assent escaped her.

J.R. couldn't help the snicker that escaped him. "I don't care about that thing, but don't you ever lie to me again. Got it?"

"Okay," Xena said.

J.R. walked to the baby who had made her way over to the statue. She had her mouth open ready to chew on it. He snatched it from her grasp before she could.

"Mine!" Kathra reached for it.

J.R. caught her by her scruff. "Forget it, you little pooper. You—hurk!" He gagged. "Holy criminy! She smells worse!" He blinked his watery eyes. "How's it possible for such a little thing to make such a big stink?"

Kathra giggled at him.

J.R. carried her to the couch. "I got the diapers. Let's get this over with." He knelt in front of her with Xena kneeling beside him. When he unclasped the tabs, he had to cover his mouth to keep from gagging. The diaper was filled with brown, lumpy . . . he didn't even want to try and figure out what was in it. "What the crap, man! What was this kid eatin'?" He held his breath and pulled a diaper out of the pack as Kathra giggled, threatening to put her foot in it. "What do I do now?"

Xena held up her hands. "I don't know how to change a diaper."

"Neither do I!" J.R. eyed the mess, hoping there was nothing moving in there.

"But you're the adult!" Xena let her arms flop. "The adult is supposed to know!"

"Sue me!" J.R. snarled. "I've never done it before."

"Hmmm . . ." Xena tapped her chin. "I watched my *Mamai* do it. First we need wipies."

"Wipies?" J.R.'s ears tilted back. "What wipies?"

"Baby wipes. They're little, wet paper things you use to wipe the baby's . . ." Xena paused. Realization washed over her as she gasped. "Oh! *That's* why they call them 'baby wipes.'"

J.R. stifled a growl. He had a sneaking suspicion he knew the answer to his next question. "Where are the wipes?"

"Didn't you get them at the store?"

J.R. pounded the couch with his fists so hard, the baby bounced. She giggled and thrust her toes in her mouth.

"You didn't tell me I needed them." J.R. eyed Xena.

Xena exhaled through her nose. "You're not very good at taking care of kids, are you, Mr. J.R.?"

The hair rose on the back of J.R.'s neck. He raised his hands to—

The doorbell rang.

"I'll get it." Xena skipped toward the door. "Oh! One time, my daddy forgot to get the wipes, and he used a wet paper towel. Maybe you can use that!" She swung around to answer the door.

"Wet paper towel, huh?" J.R. scratched his ear as he looked at Kathra contentedly sucking her toes. "Not a bad idea." His ear twitched. From somewhere deep inside a long forgotten warning stirred itself up in his mind.

"J.R.," his mother used to tell him, "don't ever answer the door to a stranger. A bad man might come to the door to steal bad, little puppies away!"

Now J.R. was old enough to question and even throw away the idea of kidnappers knocking on the door hoping a kid would answer so they could steal them away . . . at least he would have, if he didn't know some of those "bad men" personally. And some of them might actually do that. And it certainly couldn't be anyone decent coming to visit him at this time of night.

"Kid, don't answer the door!" J.R. scrambled over his feet to get to the door. He rushed to the entryway but too late. The door was already open.

CHAPTER 8

Melody pulled her sweater closer around her. It was coming on summer, but nights in these woods still got chilly. She glanced at the wipes she had shoved in the plastic shopping bag before she left home. What was she doing here, walking all this way in the middle of the night? Bringing wipes for J.R.? Why? No matter how many times she turned it over in her mind, it wasn't conceivable to her that J.R. would have a baby in his house. But, then, why the diapers?

"Maybe he's got a new artsy girlfriend who wants diapers for an art piece or somethin'." Melody snickered to herself as she walked up to J.R.'s front door. "If that's the case, this is gonna be one awkward visit." She rang the doorbell.

After a few moments of silence, the door opened.

"Hey, J—" Melody paused. A small, gray kit had answered the door.

"Hi, Miss!" She said, giving Melody a wide smile. "Can I help you?"

Melody blinked. There really was a kid in J.R.'s house. But who was she? She couldn't be any relation to J.R.—she had no sign of wolf in her, so . . .

"Um . . . hi, little girl—"

"My name's Xena."

"Xena, hi. My name's Melody. I'm looking for J.R. Can I come in?"

"No." Xena closed the door to a crack. "My *Mamai* says I'm not supposed to let strangers into the house." All Melody could see was Xena's eyes and a bit of her nose.

"Oh!" Melody bent over to get to Xena's level. "Then is your mom he—"

"Kid! What'd ya think you're doin'?" J.R.'s voice boomed. Xena's face disappeared from the crack.

Melody pushed open the door. J.R. had Xena by the scruff of her neck and was yelling in her face.

"Don't you know better than to open the door to strangers? Huh?" he barked. "You wanna get kidnapped?"

"I'm sorry." Xena had her tail between her legs.

"J.R.?" Melody stepped across the threshold.

J.R. looked up at her. "Oh, Mel. It's you." His fur settled, and he let Xena plop on the floor.

"I . . . uh . . . How . . ." Melody paused to sort through her thoughts. She had so many questions and comments all wanting to rush out of her mouth at the same time.

"What are you tryin' to say, Mel?" J.R. said.

Melody opened her mouth to try again, but the first thing that came out was, "She's too old for diapers."

There was a loud bump followed by screech.

"Kathra!" Xena rushed into the house.

"Ah! The baby!" J.R. rushed after her.

"Baby?" Melody closed the door then walked after them, removing her sweater as she did. When she joined them at the entrance to the TV room, she was struck with a horrific odor.

"My sister!" Xena shouted.

"My couch!" J.R. yelled.

"My goodness." Melody pinched her nose. A white kit was on the floor screaming while brown stains covered the couch, her hands, her feet, her tail, and her backside. A soiled diaper was still on the couch.

"She fell off the couch!" Xena swung around to J.R. "Why would you leave a baby alone on the couch? You're not supposed to do that. What if she broke her leg or something?"

"Well . . . how was I supposed to know she'd fall off?"

"You're the adult!" Xena screeched stomping her feet. "The adult is supposed to know!"

J.R. sputtered for a moment. "And . . . and what about you? You could have watched her instead of going to the door. Didn't your parents ever tell you not to open the door? This happened because you were a bad girl!"

Xena's ears fell back. Her eyes filled with tears.

Melody watched this exchange without a word. She shook her head and strode toward the baby. "There, there, little one." She picked up Kathra off the floor, mess and all. "Aw, there's nothin' wrong with you, is there? You got startled when you fell off the couch is all. Hush, now. It's alright." She rocked Kathra back and forth. Kathra looked up at her, sniffled, and quieted. "There we are. No more tears. You had a good time playin' in your mess, didn't you? But now it's time for a nice shower and a clean diaper. Wouldn't that be nice? Then you'll be all ready for bed." She carried Kathra toward the stairs. "Come on, Xena. You too. Bath time."

Xena sniffed. "Do I have to?"

"Look at you all dusty and dirty and you're asking me that question?"

"But I don't have any more clothes."

"We'll find something." Melody shot a glare at J.R. as she passed him. "You can clean up this mess."

"Are you kidding?" J.R. swung around to her. "The place is covered in crap."

"Then you should feel down right comfortable, seeing you're so full of crap yourself." Melody thrust her nose in the air as she went upstairs, leaving J.R with the stinky mess.

CHAPTER 9

"This is why I don't do nothing for no one," J.R. growled as he stood fuming at the bottom of the stairs. After he had graciously let those two brats squat in his house, all he got for his pains was numerous trips to the grocery store, dirty looks from Melody, and his stuff covered in crap. See if he'd ever do anything for anyone ever again! And the girls? No more. They were out! Out! They wouldn't spend one night here! After they were clean, he'd pack them up and drive them straight to the orphanage tonight! He'd drop them at the Lost and Abandoned Children Office. He'd dump them on the side of the road. He'd . . .

Ten minutes of fantasizing how he'd get rid of the kids wasn't getting his house clean. And he was sure Melody wouldn't do it. If he wanted his house to smell somewhat normal again, he'd have get to it himself. He stomped into the kitchen, dug around for some cleaning products at least five years old, filled a bucket with water, and got to work scrubbing. He was still cleaning when he heard Melody come down the stairs.

"Hmmm . . . I think I'll bring by some upholstery cleaner tomorrow morning." Melody stood at the entrance to the living room. "I don't think you'll be getting those stains out any more than you have."

J.R. thrust his scouring pad into the bucket of dirty water. It made his stomach churn to look at it. "Where are the brats?"

"Upstairs." Melody smiled in the direction of the steps. "The baby fell asleep right away, but Xena . . . she's so cute! She was so excited when I found one of your old shirts to wear. She really likes you, J.R."

"Lucky me." J.R. plopped on the dry side of the couch. Fantastic! He didn't want to risk waking the baby lest she let off one of those bombs again. They'd have to stay till morning.

"She insisted on praying for you before she went to sleep." Melody walked over to sit on the dry hand rest. "She said, 'Please bless Mr. J.R. Thank you for sending him to us. I'll take real good care of him.'"

"*She'll* take care of me?" J.R. said.

"That's what she said."

"She won't be 'taking care of me' for much longer." J.R. crossed his arms. "I'm gettin' rid of 'em. Tomorrow I'm dumping them at the nearest Lost and Abandoned Children Office."

Melody stood straight. "J.R., you can't do that!"

"Why not? It's where children with no parents go."

"But don't you know what happens to unclaimed children there?" Melody clutched the collar of her shirt. "They'll ship them off to Indentured Worker's Guild. They could be slaves in a matter of months!"

"Not my problem." J.R. leaned back on the couch. "They can work to pay their own way in society."

"You can't mean it! It's not their fault that . . . that . . ." Melody paused, her ears turning out. "Where did you find them, anyway? Where are their parents?"

"I found them in Jelu." J.R. ran his hands over his eyes as he remembered his first sight of them . . . a brave Kid and a half-starved baby too weak to cry. "They were sitting in the ruins. Their parents left them there."

Melody knitted her eyebrows. "Ruins? What ruins?"

"Jelu is a wasteland, Mel. It was flattened."

"How did that happen? The store just got a shipment from Jelu last week."

"The GFG Corporation were crawling around, but I didn't think they'd do that." J.R. crossed his arms. "And why would they? They just set up a branch there."

"Besides the fact they're a multi-million dollar company." Melody waved her hand. "But that's beside the point. It's not those girls' fault they got caught up in whatever happened to Jelu."

"You don't know that." J.R. turned his mouth into a pout. "Whatever their deal is, they gotta go. They'll wreck my style."

"J.R.!" Melody smacked his arm. "You're so selfish!"

"Selfish? And what about you?" J.R. glowered at Melody. "If you're so keen on them, you take 'em."

Melody opened her mouth but then shut it. She lowered her eyes.

Score one for J.R. "That's what I thought." He clicked his tongue. "I can't rid of them fast enough. Those kids are such a nuisance."

"You should reconsider, J.R."

"Why? So they can turn my life upside down? No thanks."

"J.R.—"

"Miss Melody?" A small voice said.

J.R. and Melody swung around. Xena stood at the foot of the stairs.

"You're supposed to be sleeping, Kid," J.R. let his voice lower to a growl. "Being bad again?"

"Shut up, J.R." Melody shoved him before standing up. "What are you doing out of bed, Xena?"

"I'm thirsty." Xena gave her a smile. "Can I get a drink of water?"

"Sure, sweetie. Wait there." Melody went to the kitchen.

Xena walked over to J.R. She was wearing a white shirt J.R. had overgrown, but it was so big on her the collar nearly exposed the front of her chest. Melody had tried to compensate for the size by tying the back in a knot. "Mr. J.R." She rested her elbows on his knees. "What's a noo-sains?"

"A what?"

"A noo-sains." Xena rested her head on his knees while rocking back and forth. "You said me and Kat are a noo-sains. What is that?" She tilted one of her ears, and looked up with her big eyes.

J.R. turned away to avoid being sucked in. "It's nothin' you need to worry about."

"Is it bad?"

J.R. inhaled a breath as Melody walked out of the kitchen with a glass in her hands. "Well . . . that is . . ."

"It is bad, isn't it?" Xena's ears fell. "Are you going to get rid of us too?"

"I-it's nothin' personal, Kid. But—"

Xena let her hands slide off of J.R.'s knees. "It's okay. I understand." She turned to go to the stairs, dragging her feet as she went.

"Here's your water, Xena." Melody held it out to her.

"It's okay, Miss Melody. I'm not thirsty anymore." Xena climbed up the stairs without another word.

Melody watched her go then jerked her head around to glare at J.R.

"What?" J.R. held his hands up.

Melody slammed the water on the coffee table. "I took the liberty of mixing two bottles. They're in the fridge. I don't know if the baby is old enough to sleep through the night or not, so you can give her one if she does wake up. Diapers and wipes are upstairs in the room. Don't call me in the middle of the night. You can figure it out yourself." She swung around and marched to the door.

"What are you so mad about?"

Melody picked up a bag before storming to the door.

"You don't get to give me an attitude about this, Melody!" J.R. jumped up to follow her. "I took them in; I did a good thing! And what do I get? Nothing but trouble all night long!"

Melody halted at the doorway. "You of all people should understand what they've been through—their parents leaving them behind."

"Don't bring that up now!"

"For once, J.R., I thought you were thinking about someone else!" Melody jabbed her finger into his chest. "But, no! You only think about yourself!"

"And what about you?" J.R. turned up his nose in triumph. "I notice you don't have an answer for why you won't take them in since you're so perfect!"

"I can't take them, J.R."

"Because of your oh, so interesting life opening and closing a grocery store? Face it; you don't wanna take 'em 'cause it'll ruin your life—"

"Dad's dying, J.R.!" Melody blurted.

J.R. froze. "What?"

"He's been sick for a long time." Melody wrung her fingers. "He acts fine for you, but . . . I can't take care of him and the store and two young girls at the same time. Believe me, if I could, I'd take them in a minute 'cause you don't deserve them!"

J.R. stared at her. "I . . . I . . ."

"I don't know what I expected." Melody swung around, her hair whipping through the air. "Bring 'em by before you leave. I have their clothes with me. I'd at least like to send them off with clean things." She headed down the gravel driveway.

"Y-you need a ride?" J.R. called after her.

Melody shot him a glare before she disappeared down the darkened path to the woods.

J.R. leaned on the doorway as he watched the night deepen. He growled to himself. "Doesn't change the fact they're a bother!" he said before slamming the door behind him.

CHAPTER 10

Before Celeste left the clinic, she shoved her papers under her shirt. Holding on to them as if she had a stomachache, she slowly ambled down the hall back to the slave quarters in full view of the security cameras. The way she figured it, the first thing Isha and Terrance would do once they found her missing was to look at the security cameras to see where she went. And they'd see her heading back to her room like a good, little slave. Once she reached her quarters, however, Celeste quickly changed into her only set of outdoors clothes— a gray dress, flat shoes, and a red jacket. This jacket was designed by Terrance to be as visible as possible—an extra failsafe if a slave was to escape. Celeste would have left it behind, but it was cold out here up on the mountains at night. No, she'd have to risk it and get rid of it as soon as possible. Besides, it hid the number printed on the back of her dress—the number which identified her as one of Terrance's collection.

Celeste stifled a growl as she folded her papers to stuff down her dress. She was only allowed to wear these clothes when she was sent to town for something. On those rare occasions, her shock collar would be put on a delay . . . a timer that gave her enough time to accomplish her task and get back on grounds before getting zapped. Of course, there were times when Terrance would purposely not give someone enough time to make it—usually as a

44

form of punishment. And you'd never know when or if he would do it. Being the pride of his collection, Celeste had never been on the receiving end of such treatment, but Terrance had made her learn CPR so she could resuscitate his unlucky victims.

Celeste shuddered. She'd had her lips on most of the people in the house. The ones she hadn't . . . were replacements for the ones she and Isha couldn't save.

She shoved those thoughts from her mind, eased the door open, being sure not to wake any of the other slaves sleeping in her room. As she made her way down the hall this time, she made sure to keep out of view of the cameras. Every day for the past month, she had studied how the cameras moved as she cleaned. She hadn't left any part of this escape up to chance.

Only one thing stood in her way now. Terrance's entire complex was protected by an alarm system. When Celeste first started to think about this escape plan, she didn't know how she'd get out without setting off the alarm. But one day, when she was cleaning a window, she saw how the alarm worked. The window frame had a little white thing on it with a wire running out from it. Another white thing had been placed on the part of the window that slid open and closed. When the window closed, the two white things touched. When it was open, they didn't. And that was it! At night all the doors and windows were closed which meant the white things touched. If Celeste could keep those things touching while opening the window, she could keep the alarm from going off. And she found the perfect window to try it on.

In the ball room was a little space next to the hutch which displayed the awards Terrance had won for his collection. He had placed the hutch in such a way it partially blocked one of the windows leading out to the garden. Celeste could slip in the space, open the window, and slip out without anyone seeing. Only one problem. Cameras. One of the cameras swept the space as it moved back and forth. By her count, Celeste had about twenty seconds to get in, pop the white thing off the window, open it, and slip out before the camera saw her. In preparation, she had already glued the white things together with glue she had swiped from the maintenance closet. Now, she squatted by the door out of view of the camera until the right moment. She only had one chance.

Now!

Celeste darted to the space, pried her nail behind the white thing and popped it off the window. It remained connected to its partner on the frame. Without daring to waste time looking for where the camera was, she slid open the window, jumped out, and pressed herself against the wall beneath the window. When she was certain the cameras wouldn't be on the window, she eased it shut again.

Slinking around the garden to avoid setting off the motion sensor lights or alert the guards milling about on patrol, she tip-toed to the road leading to the delivery door. There, though her freedom was a short sprint away, she sat in the bushes to wait. The road was filled with security cameras waiting to catch her flight. She'd have to wait till the morning for the next part of her plan. But for now, she had done a good night's work. She was outside without a shock collar on. Phase two of her plan was complete.

After settling down in the quiet gloom, she was aware of her stomach churning. She hadn't felt nauseous the entire time she had been trying to leave. But now in her relatively safe hiding place, her stomach heaved again—though not nearly as bad as before. Eventually, the effects of the emetic wore off, and she drifted off to sleep hidden in the bushes.

CHAPTER 11

The sun had just risen when J.R. took the Kid and the baby out to his speeder. Xena hadn't said a word all morning, but Kathra was giggling and playing with her toes like everything was roses. The two were still wearing the clothes Melody had put them in last night—bare feet and all.

Xena climbed onto the speeder's trailer, and J.R. set Kathra on her lap. Kathra laughed and tried to reach for him, but J.R. pulled his hand out of the way. No more cute looks pulling him in . . . no more attachments. All he had to do was drop them off.

"Mr. J.R.?" came Xena's voice.

"What?" J.R. put on his mirrored shades as he mounted the speeder.

"I'm sorry for being a noo-sains. I didn't mean to."

"Whatever." J.R. started his speeder. Keep a hard heart. It was time to get rid of this problem once and for all.

"Mr. J.R.?"

"What?"

Xena took a deep, shuddering breath as if she were holding back tears. "Mr. J.R., I know I'm a bad girl, and I'm sorry. You can send me away, but can you please keep Kathra?"

J.R. flipped up his shade to look at her. "What?"

"Kathra's not like me." Xena held up her sister as best as she could. "She's a good baby. Sure, she poops sometimes and cries sometimes, but she won't be bad. She's always laughing, and everybody loves her. And she likes it in your house. Whenever we go somewhere new, she cries a lot, but she went right to sleep here. She likes you, Mr. J.R. So, please. I don't want her to keep moving because of me."

J.R. pulled his shades from his snout. He was struck by her bright, brown eyes. "Kid, how old are you?"

"Five."

"Five?" J.R. turned his gaze to the woods surrounding his house. At five years old, he was too busy running around pulling girls' tails and making a mess. He didn't care two-pence about anyone else. How could she be thinking that way about her sister at her age? He clenched his teeth as a groan escaped him. He couldn't drop them off. After all, she wasn't like him whose parents had dumped him in on Mr. Withers 'cause they couldn't handle him anymore. She wasn't so bad.

He snorted and slipped his shades back on his face. "Who said I was gonna get rid of you, anyway?"

"But . . . but you said . . ." One of Xena's ears angled down. "But then where are we going?"

"You gotta eat, right?" J.R. started off.

Xena's smile stretched across her face. "Thank you, Mr. J.R." She threw her arms around his neck.

"Hey!" J.R. snarled at her. "Don't be standing up back there when I'm driving."

"Sorry." Xena sat back down. "You hear that, Kat? We get to stay!"

Kathra gave a huge laugh and kicked her feet.

J.R. watched them in the rearview, a grin crossing his face. He quickly wiped it way. "Laugh now, but this ain't no free ride, Kid. Don't know what I'm gonna do with you yet, but you better shape up and pull your weight or you're out of here. Got it?"

"Okay." Xena gave him the biggest, brightest smile he'd ever seen.

A weight slammed onto J.R.'s shoulders. He knew . . . he was certain . . . he would never be rid of these two girls for as long as he lived.

CHAPTER 12

"Hey, careful! Don't bruise them!"

"You don't gotta tell me!"

Celeste parted her eyes to the sound of shouted conversations and the roar of a truck running. She sat up. It was morning. The sun had barely risen and tinted the sky a brownish sort of pink.

"Oh, no!" Celeste's heart jumped, even as she kept her voice low. "I didn't mean to go to sleep. What time is it?"

Judging by the contents being hefted out of the delivery truck it was past 6:30. Terrance's house had a rigid schedule. Every morning the kitchen staff had to prepare to receive the day's food delivery at 6:00—feeding so many members in Terrance's "collection" took a vast amount of groceries. But the truck was the ticket to Celeste's freedom. All she had to do was slip in before anyone saw her. If only there weren't so many people watching . . .

"That's it, Joe. We're done here," said one of the delivery guys as he closed the back.

"Then get in and let's go, Stave! We've got other places to be!" said Joe, getting into the driver's seat.

Celeste gasped. What? They were done already? No . . . she had slept too long.

"Wait a minute!" said Stave. "Hey, Paulie. You didn't sign for the peaches!"

"Huh?" Paulie, one of Terrance's lackeys who watched to make sure nobody took any food from the kitchen, peeked out of the delivery door. "Ah, I know we got it. Go on!"

"Nuh, uh!" Stave marched in to the door. "The last time I let an unsigned line slide, Terrance claimed you never got the shipment and our pay got docked. Sign it."

"Fine, fine." Paulie disappeared inside with the delivery guy.

This was Celeste's chance. She darted to the truck and opened the back.

"Celeste?" the other delivery guy, Joe, approached her. "What are you doing?"

Celeste bit her lip. She had to think of something fast before he alerted somebody to her presence. "Joe . . ." She turned to face him. "I . . . uh . . ." Ooo! An idea popped into her mind. She started to breathe hard and fast and opened her eyes wide. "Joe, please let me ride in your truck. Terrance sent me into town to fetch something from the store, and . . ." She glanced around. "I don't think he's going to give me enough time to walk there and back."

"Oooo . . ." Joe flinched. "Punishment, huh? It's one of the cruelest things—not knowing if or when you'll get zapped. What'd you do?"

"I threw up on his shoes last night." Celeste let tears pool in her eyes even as she hunched over to hide her neck and her missing shock collar. "Please, Joe. I-I don't want to get shocked. Not again."

"Alright, come on." Joe beckoned to her. "Hurry before Stave see you. You can slip out when we stop."

"You're so sweet. Thanks." Celeste hopped into the back of the truck, and Joe closed it behind her.

Celeste ginned. It was so easy to make people think what you wanted them to. It was a skill she had developed growing up in Terrance's household—a way to keep or get herself out of trouble. Or to hide when she didn't want to be noticed. The only one it didn't work on was Terrance. She was too precious for him to overlook.

The truck backed up, turned, and bumped down Terrance's driveway. It slowed down as it passed Terrance's gate then took off down the main mountain street. Celeste ducked back behind one of the crates of food. She might have gotten off Terrance's property, but she wasn't safe yet. Until she got out of South

Haston, she wouldn't feel safe at all. Too many people sympathized with slave owners and empathized with the nuisance of runaway slaves. If anyone guessed she had escaped, she'd be sent right back into Terrance's clutches.

The truck stopped at its next destination. Celeste crouched further behind the crate as the door opened. She had to wait until no one was looking before she tried to slip out of the truck.

"You take care of the paperwork this time, Joe," said Stave as he opened the door. "I'll start unloading." He waited, his ear cocked to hear a response Celeste didn't catch. He burst out laughing. "I know, right?" Then he turned to the truck.

Celeste cowered in the back. She couldn't let Stave see her. He had a mean streak as wide as Terrance's.

Stave picked up a crate full of carrots and carried it outside. Celeste released her breath. With Joe handling paperwork with the client and Stave carrying the crate inside, she should be able to slip out now. She crept from her hiding place and slunk to the open door.

"Huh?" Stave appeared in the doorway, blocking the view of the parking garage they had stopped in. "What are you doing here?"

Celeste stiffened. She froze. "I . . . uh . . ."

"Wait." Stave narrowed his eyes. "That jacket . . . you're one of Terrance's, aren't you?"

"No, I'm not!" Celeste shook her head. She had to think of a lie . . . quick!

"Where's your shock collar?" Stave scratched his hair. "If you were stowing away, it should have gone off when we passed the gate."

Celeste pressed her lips together. "Um . . . I . . ."

"Wait a minute! You're trying to escape!" Stave burst into laughter. "Well, ain't this a kick!" He pulled his phone from his pocket. "Can't wait to tell ol' Terry about this one. Wonder what kind of reward he'll give me."

"No!" Celeste rushed forward before she knew what she was doing.

"No, you don't!" Stave caught her hand. "You're my meal ticket!"

"You're not taking me back!" Celeste kneed him in the groin. When he doubled over, she grabbed the biggest sack of flour she could manage and clobbered him on the side of the head. He keeled over and collapsed to the ground.

Celeste stood there panting over him with the burst bag of flour in her hands. "I didn't kill him, did I? I can't kill someone with a bag of flour, can I?"

Stave groaned. He tossed his head to the side but lay there.

Celeste breathed a sigh of relief. At once her mind kicked back into escape mode. She had to get rid of Terrance's jacket. Her original plan was to dump it after she had escaped the truck, but it would leave the number on the back of her dress exposed. But right in front of her was a better idea. She pulled Stave's delivery jacket off of him and slipped it on. Then, she dug in his wallet for money. She'd need it to make it out of town. Luckily, his wallet was full of bills.

She stuffed the money into the jacket pocket and tossed the wallet back on him. "Thanks for the help, Stave." She gave him a kick to the side before darting to the street. She ran straight for the nearest bus station, bought a ticket, and waited for the bus, hoping no one would notice her fur. When her bus came, she jumped on without a moment's hesitation.

As the bus pulled away from the station, Celeste grinned ear to ear. She had done it. She had escaped. Next stop: Jelu and freedom.

CHAPTER 13

Melody had never been so furious for so long in her entire life. Not only had J.R. neglected to bring Xena and Kathra the morning he was going to drop them off at the Lost Children Office, but he had ignored every, single call she had made. Plus, he had been avoiding her since then. The three times she had gone over there, he refused to answer the door. Not only was he selfish; he was a coward.

She growled as she shoved mason jars into a bag for one of her customers. That J.R.! When she saw him next, he was dead!

"Uh, Melody?"

"What?" Melody snarled at Betton Darson, a possum and one of her dear friends.

"You're cracking the jars." Betton pulled a jar out of the bag. It had a long, white crack down the side.

"Sorry, Bet." Melody handed her another to replace it.

"What's got your tail in a knot?" Betton handed Melody a bill. "Never mind the bagging. I'll do it."

"Ugh! It's J.R." Melody pounded the button on the cash register. "He's been avoiding me for four days now!"

"Oh!" Betton bagged the rest of the jars. "Speaking of J.R., have you heard what people are sayin' about him? They say he's—"

"I don't want to hear nothing about him." Melody held up her hand. "I'm so mad at him, I could spit."

"You'll make up soon." Betton scooped up her bag. "It's the sort of relationship you have."

"Not this time." Melody handed Betton her change. "What he did was unforgivable."

"We'll see." Betton turned to leave. "Speak of the devil . . . hey, J.R."

"Mornin', Bett." J.R. held the door open for her. "You are lookin' scrumptious today."

"Ooo, you gonna make my husband jealous." Betton waved her hand in front of her face.

"He better be." J.R. gave her a toothy grin. "I'm gonna get you one of these days." He clopped his teeth together.

"You so bad, J.R. My, my. I better go before I get impure thoughts." Betton fanned herself and muttered, "Andra's right. How can anyone can be so evil and hot at the same time?"

Melody rolled her eyes. Betton couldn't whisper if her life depended on it.

"Bye, Melody. I—" Betton halted mid-sentence, her eyes drifting downward on something behind J.R. "Oh. What—?"

"Don't bother." J.R. waved her off.

Melody didn't get a chance to see what stopped Betton's stream of gossip and banter. As soon as J.R. looked at her, she turned her back on him.

"What's wrong with you, Mel?" J.R. frowned at her. "You've got on a face that could sour milk."

"As if you don't know!"

"Aw, you're not mad I didn't return your calls, are ya?" J.R. rolled his eyes. "Didn't know you were so clingy."

"Well, hello there, little ones," Betton said, her voice carrying over Melody's rage. "What 'cha doing following J.R. around? Where're your parents?"

Silence fell for a moment before a small, clear, high-pitched voice yelled, "Stranger! Stranger! Stranger!"

Melody swung around. Xena stood at the door to the grocery store, holding Kathra's hand as she toddled along. Xena was pointing at Betton and continued yelling like a siren, "Stranger! Stranger! Stranger!"

Betton, for her part, kept trying to shush Xena even as everyone in the store stared and snickered.

"Knock it off, Kid." J.R. leaned on the counter. "She ain't no stranger."

"Oh. Okay." Xena smiled at Betton. "Sorry, Miss." She turned to face the counter. "Hi, Miss Melody."

"Xena?" Melody rushed from behind the counter. "What are you doing here? Hi, baby!" She picked up Kathra. "Aw, you smell so nice today."

"We took a bath." Xena swayed back and forth, her fur catching the light.

"I see. Your fur looks so shiny and clean." Melody sighed. "Why is it kids have the best fur? Look at how beautiful it is. Can't get my fur that shiny, no matter what beauty products I use."

J.R. shrugged.

"Um." Betton stood at the door. "Isn't anybody gonna tell me what's going on? Where'd those kids came from?"

"Melody? What's all the racket down here?" Mr. Withers, a brown Manchester terrier, ambled down the stairs into the store. His ears drooped at the ends, and gray speckled his fur—quite a change from the strong dog pictured in all the family photos upstairs. Still, he was dressed in the green apron he required everyone who worked in the store to wear.

"Dad, you should be in bed." Melody rushed over to catch his arm and help him walk.

"Ah, get off! I ain't an invalid!" Mr. Withers turned his nose up at Kathra still in Melody's arms. "Who's this?"

"This is Kathra." Melody bounced the baby. "And over there is Xena."

"Hi, mister." Xena grinned over the counter, though she was barely tall enough to see over it.

Mr. Withers bent over to look her in the eye. "And why are you making so much noise?"

"A stranger was trying to talk to me." Xena pointed to Betton still at the door.

"What you doing hanging around with the door half open, Bett?" Mr. Withers shook his head. "You weren't raised in a barn."

"I want to know what's going on here."

"You got preservin' to do today, don't cha? Get going." Mr. Withers sighed. "You'll hear the whole story by night's end, most likely."

Betton pouted. "But I wanted to be the first."

"Go on with ya!" Mr. Withers shooed her out.

"Fine. Talk to you later, Mel." Betton walked out, looking at J.R. through the window as she went.

Mr. Withers shook his head. "Got a bigger mouth than a gator. Now, you two." He turned his attention to Xena. "What's your story? What'd you come here for?"

"We came to go shopping!" Xena said.

J.R. snorted through his nose. "The Kid's always whining about something. 'We need clothes; we need shoes; we need toys!' Ugh! Today she's whining about groceries."

"Because there's never any food in the house!" Xena put her hands on her hips.

"Sounds about right," Melody said.

J.R. turned up his nose. "I feed you, don't I?"

"My *Mamai* says too much fast food isn't good for you," Xena said.

"Enough with the '*Mamai*' crap. It's 'mommy', alright? Say it right." J.R. shook his head. "Never seen such a health conscious kid before. Care to help me out, Mel. Not sure what all we need."

"I can do it!" Xena held up a piece of paper. "I made a list."

"A list?" J.R. snatched it from her. "Is this what you were scribbling all morning?"

"Don't grab." Melody pulled it from his grasp. It was filled with words written in giant, uneven letters. "Did you write this all by yourself?"

"So we wouldn't forget anything. The adult's supposed to remember but . . ." Xena beckoned to Melody. ". . . but Mr. J.R. is not a very good adult," she whispered in her ear.

Melody snickered.

"What'd you say?" J.R. said.

Xena gave him a huge grin. "Nothing."

J.R. narrowed his eyes at her. "You lyin' to me again?"

Xena's eyes grew wide. She bit her lips together, then turned to Melody. "Can we go shopping now?"

"Sure." Melody set Kathra in the cart. "What's on your list?"

"Let's see . . ." Xena hopped on the back of the cart and looked at her list as Melody pushed. "We need eggs and cereal . . . oh, and milk for Kathra . . . and we need candy and milk and cheese crackers and . . . Oh! I didn't put peanut butter and jelly."

"So you like peanut butter?" Melody said, making faces at the baby as she pushed.

"Yup. My daddy taught me how to make good peanut butter and jelly sandwiches." Xena bent over backward to look at J.R. "I'll make you some for lunch, okay, Mr. J.R.?"

J.R. raised his eyebrows. "You're cooking? 'Bout time I got something out of this deal."

"You're a lowlife, J.R.," Melody said.

"Thank you," J.R. said.

Melody rolled her eyes in disgust and pushed the cart to leave him behind.

CHAPTER 14

J.R. watched Melody push the cart and the two girls away. He collapsed against the counter with a sigh. This was the first time in four days he had gotten any peace. The kid would not shut her yapper.

"Yup, that's the look most first time parents give me." Mr. Withers leaned on the counter so his face was next to J.R.'s.

"I ain't their dad."

Mr. Withers chuckled.

"So, how you feelin', Old Man?" J.R. lifted his head. "Melody says you were real sick."

"I'm fine. Melody's a worrier—like her ma." Mr. Withers stretched his back. "True, I would've been back on my feet days ago if I was a younger dog, but . . . bah!" He shrugged.

It was J.R.'s turn to chuckle.

"So what's the story with the kits?" Mr. Withers leaned his elbows on the counter. "Where'd they come from?"

"I found them in the pile of rubble that used to be Jelu."

Mr. Wither's eyes widened, exaggerating the wrinkles surrounding them. "Melody said something similar, but I thought she was exaggerating."

"Musta happened right before I got there." J.R. shook his head. "It was still smoking."

"What were you doing there?"

"Had a job," J.R. said, and left it at that. Neither Mr. Withers nor Melody approved of his line of work. And judging by the way Mr. Withers grunted, he still didn't.

J.R. labelled himself a Master Thief—able to liberate anything from anywhere without anyone realizing it was missing. In fact, his trip to Jelu had been to relieve a priceless holo-disk from a bank vault. But the bank, buildings, everything had been levelled. J.R. had been about to search through the bank ruins to find the disk when he had met Xena and Kathra.

"What do you think happened?"

"Dunno. I can't think of what could level the entire city." J.R. stroked his chin. "We're not far from Jelu. If a bomb went off, we should have heard or seen something."

"And there's been nothing about it on the news."

"Plus, how did the kids survive?" J.R. watched Melody take the girls up one aisle and then the other. "I want to go back to investigate, but the GFG Corporation has already moved in to rebuild."

"The GFG Corporation? Not the government?"

"From what I understand, they greased a lot of palms for the privilege." J.R. sniffed. "They're searching for something."

"What?"

"Dunno, but it might be what caused the city to collapse. They're always experimenting with different technologies . . . dabbling in military applications. Nothing like this though."

"Ah, boy!" Mr. Withers ran his hand over his face. "So, what are you going to do with the kits?"

J.R. stared at the spinning fan a moment. "Guess I'm gonna keep 'em."

"You? Taking care of two little girls?" Mr. Withers burst into laughter.

J.R. didn't move. "If anyone would have told me that last week, I would have laughed then punched them."

"You're serious, then?" Mr. Withers smile faded. "You're going to keep them?"

"I don't have a choice."

"What do you mean?"

"Because the kid . . . she . . . I don't know." J.R. felt his fur rise. "She has this power over me."

"What?"

Before he could answer, J.R. felt a tug on his coat. When he looked down, he spied Xena holding up a box of cookies. "Mister J.R., can I get this, too? Please?" She grinned so wide it made her squint.

J.R. knew it was a mistake to look into her adorable, wide brown eyes. He'd get lost in the innocence of the gold flashes and her bright smile. He knew it, but he did it anyway. Before he was aware, he found himself saying, "Sure, you can, Kid. Get anything you want."

Xena jumped up and down. "Thank you, Mr. J.R." She hugged his leg before hopping around a corner.

"There's what I mean," J.R. said. "Every time I'm convinced I should give them up, the kid does or says something so blasted cute I can't say 'no' to her." He hit his head on the counter. "I'm going soft."

"Like a marshmallow."

"I can't do this." J.R. shook his head. "I haven't gotten a good night's sleep in four days. Not to mention the baby . . . her diapers are worse than chemical warfare. And what am I supposed to do when I have a date?"

"Having kids is a big decision. They'll change everything."

"I'd probably kill them within a week."

Mr. Withers fingered his chin. "Probably less."

"I'm not like you . . . a responsible adult who has successfully raised a beautiful daughter and straightened out a delinquent kid."

"Not sure about how straight the delinquent kid is . . ." Mr. Withers eyed J.R. "But what are you getting at?"

"Can you take them? For a little while?" J.R. clasped his hands. "Please."

"No, no, no." Mr. Withers faked a cough. "I'm a sick, old man. I'm too frail to handle kids."

"Just until I finish my pending jobs. Three weeks . . . a month, max."

"No."

"Alright." J.R. straightened his coat. "I'll go to plan B."

"What's plan B?"

J.R. smirked, ears falling slightly. "Use their cuteness against you."

"I've already raised kids." Mr. Withers rested his cheek on his hand. "I'm immune to cuteness. Plan C?"

"Bribery."

"Plan D?"

"Blackmail."

"Plan E?"

"Threatening."

Mr. Withers laughed out loud. "I've known you since you were a pup. I'm not afraid of you." He struck his fist in his palm. "And I can still take you over a knee. Plan F?"

"Merciless begging." J.R. dropped to his knees.

"Plan G?"

J.R. raised his hands. "That's all I've got."

"Then you're out of luck," Mr. Withers said.

"These girls are so cute!" Melody approached, pushing a cartload of groceries. Kathra kicked her feet and burst into laughter every time her heel hit the grocery cart. Melody stopped to look down at J.R. "What are you doing on the floor?"

"Unsuccessfully asking your father for a favor." J.R. stood to brush his knees off. "What's all this?"

"Essentials." Melody unloaded the cart for Mr. Withers to ring up. "And you're paying for all of it."

"This is robbery of a kind even I would never stoop to," J.R. muttered.

Melody snickered.

"Hey, where's the Kid?" J.R. looked around, but Xena was nowhere to be seen.

"Over in the corner." Melody pointed with her chin. "She wanted to draw, so I let her open a pack of pens and an activity book."

J.R. stiffened his whiskers. "I guess I have to pay for them too?"

"It's on me." Melody chuckled. "She was so cute when she asked with her big ol' brown eyes."

"See, Withers? It's not just me." J.R. glared at Xena, lying on her stomach drawing. "Look at her sitting there, plotting her next move. She knows what she's doing. It's a setup."

"You've been a fugitive too long, J.R.," Melody said. "You're getting paranoid."

"$274.59," Mr. Withers said.

"For groceries?"

"You live off of nothing but alcohol and crackers," Melody said.

J.R. grumbled as he removed his wallet and handed him the money.

"Done!" Xena skipped over to J.R. "I made something for you, Mr. J.R." She held out her drawing to him.

J.R. looked at it. Three stick figures, each with ears and a tail, stood in front of a square and triangle house. A swirling smoke stack ascended from a non-existent chimney. Above it all was a thing with wings.

"Criminy, Kid. I already said you can stay." J.R. snarled at her. "This is overkill, ain't it?"

"Huh?" Xena's ears fell. "I . . . um . . . you don't like it?"

J.R. glanced at his companions. "Watch this. After this, you'll see she knows exactly what she's doing." He picked up Xena and set the picture on the counter. "Tell them what it is."

Xena pointed to the biggest stick figure. "That's you . . ." She pointed to the medium one. ". . . and that's me . . ." She pointed to the smallest one. ". . . and that's Kat." She pointed to the thing with wings. "And that's an angel. He's happy because you're going to take care of us." She smiled so that her nose crinkled.

Melody covered her mouth and squealed, "That's so adorable!"

Mr. Withers turned to hide his laughter.

"Do you like it?" Xena looked up at him with her eyes wide.

"Yeah, Kid. It's nice."

Xena threw her arms around him.

J.R. looked at Mr. Withers and mouthed, "And that is why I'll never be able to get rid of her." He set Xena down, and walked out with the groceries, still in the cart.

CHAPTER 15

"I do not want your excuses, Squall! I want results!" Max's voice echoed across the rubble. Perched atop a pile of rubbish that must have been twenty or thirty feet high, the red fox had a good vantage point to watch a squad of his men picking through the ruins of Jelu for the thirtieth time. To his right stood a surveyor, pointing his instruments to measure the landscape.

"I know, sir, but they kept moving it; it wasn't my fault," said the black ferret standing in front of him. Max rolled his eyes and allowed them to wander across the ruined landscape as the ferret yammered on with a boring and pointless excuse. It was all the same to him. At the end of the day, all his excuses meant he had failed.

Max pulled his yellow hard hat off his head and smoothed his red hair. "I don't know if I can handle this incompetence anymore," he said, causing Squall to stop talking. "How hard could it be to pick it up? I practically gift-wrapped it." He took to massaging the bridge of his nose.

"Sir . . ." Squall fiddled with the tail of his orange construction shirt. Everyone, even Max, had to wear the vest and hard hat in these ruins. "I . . . can do the job . . . if you give me another chance?"

"Another chance?" Max glared at Squall. "You've had three

weeks of chances, and . . . you know what? Get out of my sight. I can't handle you right now."

Squall whimpered but turned to scramble down the rubble pile.

Max blew a breath out of his mouth. Squall had been the latest recruit to his "Board of Advisors," a fancy term referring to those people closest to him in his company. They were the only ones who knew he was looking for something here in Jelu . . . and most of them didn't even know what they were really looking for. But Squall knew. He knew, but after this failure Max couldn't trust him again. He certainly couldn't trust him to keep it secret.

"This is so annoying." Max drew his gun from his jacket holster, aimed at Squall's retreating form, and pulled the trigger. A white laser streaked through the air and struck Squall in the back of his head. He dropped where he stood.

Max exhaled a loud breath while cracking his neck. "Yeah, that made me feel better. Hey, Jordan! Jané!" He looked to a leopard and a black panther standing about halfway down the rubble. He beckoned to them as they turned.

"'Sup, Boss?" Jané got to Max first. She walked with a smooth, almost oily motion that reminded Max of a snake.

Jordan stopped to examine Squall's body before joining Max. "What's happening?"

"I'm going to have to write a nice obituary for Squall." Max pointed at the body with his chin.

"Couldn't retrieve the package, huh?" Jordan sniffed.

Jané chuckled. "You should have sent Jordan and me."

Max ignored her. "I'm thinking about something like . . . he was a good worker, an invaluable member of the team . . . yadda, yadda, blah, blah. But his most tragic death was caused by a . . ." He motioned to Jané to fill in the blanks.

"Where'd you get him?"

"Back of the head." Max tapped the spot on his own head.

Jordan squinted at Squall's body. "No blood there."

"The gun was set pretty high." Max sniffed. "Cauterized the wound."

"Hmmm . . ." Jané scanned the rubble. "There's a lot of unstable debris that could . . ." She rapped her knuckles on her head. ". . . conk him on the head."

"Ah, perfect!" Max clapped his hands together. "Another

unfortunate victim of Jelu."

"And people will go for that?" Jordan asked. "There's a laser burn on the back of his head."

Jané shrugged. "As long as we don't give anyone a reason to run an autopsy. We can hide the burn."

"Great." Max pointed his clasped hands at her. "Take care of it for me?"

"Will do, Boss." Jané winked at him as she descended the rubble.

"Oh, and, Jané, make sure all our permits are in order." Max called after her. "I want us to be the only ones doing restorations on this town."

Jané paused halfway down the rubble. "Is the government going to be okay with it?"

"As long as the paperwork is in order and I'm footing this bill, no one will care," Max shouted. "So make sure it's done right."

"Yeah, Boss!" Jané pointed in the air as descended the rubble toward Squall.

"What a mess!" Max surveyed the damage once again. Everything for miles around had been flattened.

Jordan shook his head. "What happened here?"

"No idea." Max massaged the bridge of his nose again. As the founder and CEO of the GFG Corporation, Max felt the pressure of the Board of Directors baring down on him. Jelu represented a significant investment on his part, and it had crumbled in one night. "Terrance Claybourne must be having a field day. How am I going to recover from this?"

"We could start by actually clearing the rubble."

"Not yet." Max took a breath as he surveyed his team working. "Tess and her team are making one more pass."

"What are you searching for?"

"A disk. And Squall's missing package."

"Which is?"

"Doesn't matter. Doesn't look like it's here anymore." Max growled in his throat. "If Squall wasn't already dead, I'd kill him."

"All this is doing nothing for our timeline."

"You're right." Max chewed on the inside of his cheek a moment. "Once Tess's team is finished this pass, get ready to clear the rubble. Get us back on schedule."

"Will do." Jordan's ears pricked as the sound of sliding stones reached Max's ears.

Max turned. A gray vixen clambered up the pile of rubble toward them. As she scaled the top, her foot slipped on the loose stones. Max caught her before her face smacked the dirt.

"Oh, thank you." The vixen looked up at him with the biggest green eyes Max had ever seen.

Max set her on her feet as he let his eyes rove over her from ears to tail. He had never seen a vixen with gray fur in real life. Pictures of them, sure, but all the foxes he knew had red fur like his. And her chin length hair was so black it almost looked blue. She wore a dress that did nothing for her shape, a jacket belonging to some food delivery place, and flat shoes not meant for walking very far. He could imagine the blisters she must have on her toes. But all told, not a bad looking girl. If he cared about that sort of thing. Which he didn't.

"Get on with your work, Jordan," Max said. "I'll take care of this."

"Sure." Jordan glanced at her before walking away.

"Who are you?" Max turned his eyes away from the vixen.

The vixen stood straight. "My name is Celeste."

"Uh, huh." Max didn't spare her another glance. "And what are you doing here?"

"I—"

"Ah, forget it. I don't need to know." Max waved her off. "It's not safe here. You need to wear a hardhat and safety vest to be in this area."

"I will leave, but . . . can you help me?" Celeste spun in a circle. "I think I'm lost."

"I'll say you are. But . . . wait." Max turned to her. "How'd you get passed the roadblock I set up around the whole town?"

"Um . . . it's a long story . . ." Celeste twirled her fingers in her hair. "But it involves hitchhiking, batting my eyes, and getting a poor sap to do me a favor." She hissed in a breath. "Sure hope the angry bat that rushed at him wasn't his wife." She gave Max a sly sort of smile.

Max couldn't help the snicker that escaped him. "That's kinda funny."

"I thought so too." Celeste held her hands behind her back.

"What are you looking for, then?"

"The GFG Corporation's office. One's supposed to be in Jelu, but . . . this can't be the right place."

"The GFG Corporation?" Max pointed to a pile of concrete toward the east. "It's right around there."

"Huh?"

"Look around, girl. The whole place is destroyed." Max sighed as his ears fell. "Everything . . . my offices, my employees . . . all gone. This was supposed to be my town. Whoever did this is going to pay!"

"But . . . but this can't be Jelu . . ." Celeste seemed to shrink as she looked over the rubble. "I . . . I have to get to the GFG. I have to!"

"What do you want with them? Looking for a job?"

"Oh, no, sir." Celeste turned her back to him and turned back with a piece of paper in her hands. "I want to join the Freedom Project."

Max took the paper. It was one of the ads he had run in a magazine. He lifted a scrutinizing eye to her. "You're a slave?"

"Yes, sir."

Max sighed. "Sorry, but I think we're going to have to suspend the initiative for a while."

"But you can't—"

"Do you see this?" Max opened his arms to indicate the rubble all around him. "This represents millions of dollars my company just lost. And millions, possibly billions, I'm going to need to restore and repair this place. Something has to give!"

"But I can't go back to Terrance!" Celeste clutched the collar of her dress. "He'll kill me for running away . . . or something worse!"

"Terrance?" Max's ears shot straight up. "Terrance Claybourne? The Collector?"

Celeste nodded.

"You're his?"

Celeste pressed her lips together and nodded.

"And you escaped? To come here?"

Celeste nodded.

Max stroked his chin. Terrance Claybourne had been a thorn in his side since he had started the Freedom Project . . . using his money and influence to back Max's competitors and attempting to block the GFG from lucrative contracts, undercutting his business, sending corporate spies or people to steal from him. To get even with Terrance Claybourne . . . a smile slipped onto his face. This chance was too good to pass up.

"Tell me, Celeste. What did you do for Terrance?"

"I worked in the house . . . cooked, cleaned . . . things like that." Celeste took to unconsciously stroking the fur on her arm. "But what he really used me for is showing off. I was the pride of his collection."

"Of course. A gray-furred red fox." Max nodded. "Very rare."

Celeste's ears angled backward. "I know."

"Hmm . . ." Max stroked his chin as he studied her. "This could work for me . . . you've got a pretty face . . ."

"Oh." Celeste smiled at him as color came to her cheeks. "Thank you."

"I was stating a fact." Max held up a hand. "I didn't mean for it to be construed as romantic interest in any way."

"Oh . . . okay." Celeste cocked her head. "But what's 'construed' mean?"

"Forget it." Max waved her off.

"Max!" Tess, a brown weasel, jumped up and down at him from her spot in front of a half-ruined wall. "We found something!"

"Come on, Celeste. Stay with me until I figure out what to do with you." Max took a step before snapping his fingers. "Oh, you're going to need a hardhat." He plopped his hat on her head before sliding down the rubble pile. "What did you find?"

"This." Tess opened her hand. In it was a clump of gray fur. Max picked it up. It shimmered as he rolled it between his fingers. A grin spread across his face. "I don't believe it. The legends are true."

"Sure looks like it."

Max gripped the fur in his fist. "Please tell me you have some good news about what happened."

"I've got better than good news." Tess used the tablet in her hands to point. "We found tracks headed to the road and evidence of a vehicle leaving."

"So she's alive." Max put a hand to his head. "What a relief. Any clue where she went?"

"That's where my good news ends, I'm afraid." Tess shrugged.

"Anyone could have picked her up. She might even be a slave by now."

"If she is, she'd be fairly easy to find."

"I'll run a search with the Estate Office." Tess tapped it into her tablet.

"What about the disk?"

Tess slapped a black, plastic, rectangular disk in his hand. "Was in the bank vault—or the remains of it—like our contact said."

"I hope whatever destroyed Jelu didn't harm it." Max pulled a portable holodisk player from his pants pocket.

"Don't bother. I already checked it. Most of the data is corrupted. It's no good to us anymore."

"Blast!" Max crushed the disk in his bare hands.

Celeste appeared beside him. "What . . . a steep hill . . ." She rested her hands on her knees and panted.

"Who's this?" Tess studied Celeste up and down.

"Her name's Celeste." Max let the holodisk pieces fall from his hand.

"Nice to meet you, Celeste." Tess held out her hand for Celeste to shake it.

Celeste stared at her hand a moment. With a small smile, she took Tess's hand. "Hi."

"She wants to be a part of the Freedom Project." Max dusted off his hands.

Tess inhaled a breath through clenched teeth. "I don't know, Max. With all this going on, do you think the company will fund it?"

"I'll pay for it myself if I have to." Max studied Celeste. "She says she's Terrance Claybourne's pride. If it's true, she's worth her weight in gold."

Celeste snorted through her nose with her mouth pinched, though she said nothing else. Perhaps she had heard people speak about her like this before.

"Should be easy to check." Tess tapped on her tablet and swiped the screen a few times. "Looks like you're right, Max! She was on the cover of his magazine two months ago." She hit a button, and a holographic display of *Collector's Monthly* magazine appeared in the air. Celeste was on the cover, her fur brushed to a shine, and her hair smoothed in place.

Celeste gasped. "So that's why he had me take all those pictures."

"She's very photogenic." Max examined the photo.

"Photo . . . genic?" Celeste looked from Max to Tess. "Is that good?"

"It's very good." Tess smiled at her. "It means you take nice pictures. And it's true; look at these." She turned the hologram so that Celeste could see it better. "You look lovely."

Celeste put her hands to her heart. "Thank you."

"But you have got to be expensive. If you're Terrance's pride, I can't see him setting your list price very low." Tess tapped the button and the picture disappeared. "Are you sure you want to use your own money to do this, Max?"

"The money isn't the problem for me." Max stroked his chin. "But getting access to her papers will be next to impossible."

"I have my papers." Celeste turned her back on him to reveal crumpled papers when she turned back.

"You came prepared for everything." Max smoothed them out and examined them. He inhaled a breath through clenched teeth. "$650,000."

Tess whistled. "Steep."

"Worth it, though." Max grinned. "She'll be the new face of the Freedom Project. Can you imagine what will happen when everyone sees that even the pride of Terrance's collection can be freed by us?"

"You mean, besides Terrance blowing his stack?" Tess winked at Celeste.

"That's worth it in and of itself, but imagine all the free publicity we'll get! Anti-slavery groups will be throwing money at us." Max rubbed his hands together. "And if I can play this right, I can get other companies to sponsor it. It'll be a goldmine!" He looked around at the ruin. "It will subsidize the rebuilding of Jelu. The company won't lose another dime."

"Considering everything goes according to plan," Tess said.

"Everything goes according to my plans eventually, Tess." Max straightened his jacket. "Take Celeste down to the Estate Office right away. Once she's taken care of, I'll have our PR girl set her up with the photographers and marketers to get a new Freedom Project campaign running."

"On my way." Tess turned Celeste around. "Come on, Celeste. You're going to love working for us. We . . ." Her voice faded into the distance.

Max turned as Tess and Celeste walked away. So far everything had turned out okay today; he had managed to turn everything around. Perhaps he hadn't needed to kill Squall.

He paused to mull it over. Actually, yeah. Yeah he did.

CHAPTER 16

J.R. heard the wood settling. It was a homey, comforting sound; a sound he had never noticed before. Noises like this, what J.R. called "quiet noises," were things he had come to treasure with the "Kid" and the "Kat" around. Over the last three weeks, they had completely overtaken the upper floors. Toys were all over the ground. Kid shows on TV. Baths every other day. There was no end to it.

But he was his own man in his basement. He had converted it into a workroom and gym separated by dry wall. In his workroom he kept a workbench, some tools and scanners scattered here and there, and some books and other equipment tossed on shelves. His gym was covered in gymnast mats. A weight set sat in one corner and in another hung a punching bag and a heavy bag.

Right now, he sat hunched over his workbench and tinkered with a gadget he had gotten. It was square, metal box that had an ammeter built into it to detect the flow of electricity. A light bulb was screwed into the top. The entire thing was connected to a volt/ohm meter, which J.R. was using to test it. The machine was designed to channel a person's bioelectricity from a disk attached to the arm, through the wire, and into the metal box, thus turning on the light bulb. However, J.R. had not been able to make the sensors strong enough to pick up the minute amounts of bioelectricity the body generates.

He heard tiny footsteps hopping down the stairs. "I said you weren't allowed down here, Kid."

Xena's face appeared in the doorway. "You said I couldn't come down here without you, and you're here now." She skipped over to him.

"Where's your sister?"

"She's sleeping. She sleeps a lot." She climbed up on his lap, settled in, and rested her chin in her hands. "I'm bored, Mr. J.R. I don't want to watch TV anymore."

J.R. had to smile. This girl had some nerve, and he respected that.

As she examined the items on the workbench, the light caught her fur and made it glisten. J.R. had noticed—especially after Melody mentioned it in the store—that Xena's fur looked shinier than anyone else's he knew.

"What are you doing, Mr. J.R.?" Xena asked, using both hands to pick up an electric meter.

"Don't touch it!" J.R. snatched it from her and tried to stretch around her to keep working. "I'm doing a favor for a friend."

"What favor?"

"Trying to get this to work." J.R. tapped the gadget with his screwdriver.

"What's it supposed to do?"

"Use bioelectricity to turn on a light bulb. He can't get it to work, so he asked me to look at it."

"What's bio . . . what's that?"

"Electricity your body makes."

"Oh." Xena examined the machine. "Why can't he work it?"

"I don't know." J.R. chewed on the end of the screwdriver. Tinkering with electronics wasn't his forte, but the idea of this gadget—using the body's electricity to power a machine . . . only having to think about what you wanted the machine to do and the machine responding—was intriguing. Imagine all the ways he could use this in his line of work. But . . . "Why won't this stupid thing work?"

Xena looked up at him with a slight pout. "You're not supposed to say 'stupid.'"

"Shut up."

"You're not supposed to say 'shut up,' either," Xena muttered. But she didn't say anything louder. Instead she studied the gadget again. "Can I try to turn on the light?"

"Why not?" J.R. strapped the disk on Xena's arm. No harm in letting her try it if it would keep her quiet a few minutes. After all, he was sure it wasn't dangerous . . . pretty sure . . . he'd tried it a million times, and nothing had happened to him. Sure, she was smaller, but . . .

Xena squealed and jumped, and J.R.'s heart leapt into his throat. "I did it!" she said.

J.R. looked at the light bulb. It was dark.

"Watch." Xena looked at the bulb, balled her fists, and squeezed her eyes shut. Sweat started to bead on her forehead, and she trembled as she concentrated. The light bulb flickered on and went out when she relaxed. "It's hard."

J.R. gazed at her. Here, a five-year-old accomplished in two seconds what he had spent two years trying to do. "How did you do that?"

Xena shrugged.

J.R. took the sensor off of Xena and strapped it to his arm. He stared at the light bulb, clenched his fists, and willed it to turn on, but it remained dark. He stood, making Xena fall off of his lap, gripped the table, and glared at the thing so hard his knuckles went white and his tail stood on end. Still the stupid thing refused to work. "You little—"

"Maybe it doesn't like you," Xena said.

J.R. glared at her, his tail stiffening. "Don't you have something else to do?"

"No." She hugged his leg. "I want to be with you."

J.R. rolled his eyes. He turned back to his gadget and ignored her. Perhaps she would get bored and leave.

Xena watched him for a moment and then held her hands behind her back and rocked back and forth. Then she spun around in circles and laughed as her skirt flew up. After doing this thirteen times—J.R. counted, for each giggle made him lose his concentration and made him clench his teeth a little harder—she played imaginary hop-scotch, and hopped toward the door leading to his gym.

"Oooh!" Xena peered inside. "Mr. J.R., what's in there?"

J.R. didn't move, but felt his eyebrows knit. "My gym."

"A gym! Do you do excerseses in there?" Xena started jumping up and down and clapping her hands. "1 . . . 2 . . . 3 . . . 4 . . ."

J.R. clutched the table and forced his ears to stand back up. "I don't do exercises in there."

"Then what do you do in there?" Xena asked.

"I practice fighting," J.R. said through his teeth.

"Fighting?" Xena's eyes grew wide. "Fighting's bad."

"Not when you're trying to defend yourself."

Xena cocked her head. "Why do you have to?"

J.R. took a deep breath and let it out slowly, aware his nails were piercing his palms and his ears were lying flat against his skull. "Because."

"Because why?"

J.R. bit his lip. "Because."

"Because why?"

J.R. shot up, grabbed her by both arms, and shook her as hard as he could. "Xena, shut up!" He released her so hard she had to take two steps backwards to regain her balance. When she did, she gazed at him with wide eyes.

Xena's mouth screwed up in a pout. "You're so *mean!*" She shoved him as hard as she could before turning her back on him and plopping cross-legged on the floor.

J.R. snorted through his nose. She might have been mad, but at least she was quiet. Maybe now he'd be able to get back to work. With a sigh, he sat back in his chair.

But in all his life, J.R. had never been able to stand being in the same room with an angry female . . . even one as small as Xena. Her rage kept buzzing at him like an angry bee. He couldn't stand it anymore.

"Would you stop pouting?" J.R. swung around in his chair.

"No, you're mean!"

"Would someone mean get you all that candy upstairs?"

"You yelled at me. I didn't even do anything!"

"Because you're too loud. You're asking too many questions. I want some quiet."

Xena peeked over her shoulder at him. "You don't want me to ask questions?"

"Just be quiet, okay?" J.R. put a finger to his lips. "Shh."

A smile broke through Xena's pout. "Okay."

"Thank you." J.R. turned back to his project.

Xena sat where he left her, playing with her toes and not making a sound. Perhaps now he could finally get some work done.

He picked up his gadget and started to open the casing.

"Mr—oops." Xena clapped her hands over her mouth. "Sorry."

J.R. turned his attention back to the casing but felt the unasked question buzzing in the air, crashing into his mind over and over like a fly trapped on a screened-in porch. "What, Kid?"

"But you don't want me to ask—"

J.R. gripped the screwdriver. "Just ask."

"Can I go in your gym?"

J.R. flung the door open. "Don't touch the weights." He watched her run in, and then went back to his gadget. He removed the casing and examined the multicolored wires crisscrossing each other. Perhaps one of them needed to be replaced with something more conductive. Maybe an alloy take that, you meanie . . . J.R. pricked his ears and looked up. What had come over him?

"Go away, you!" Xena's voice floated out of his gym and circled the air around his head. He rolled his eyes and tried to turn his attention back to his project, but Xena's voice flew through the air and burrowed into his thoughts until she was all he could hear. He laid his head on the table, and covered his ears with both hands. Still Xena's voice came through.

J.R. threw his hands into the air and groaned. "She doesn't shut up."

"Take that!" Xena shouted. "You leave Mr. J.R. alone, you bad man!"

J.R. lifted his head. He rose and peeked into the gym.

Xena lunged at the heavy bag with all her might, but the kickback knocked her onto her tail. "Mr. J.R. is my friend. Go away!" She jumped up and gave it a punch that didn't even make it move.

"No, no. You're doing it wrong." J.R. set her aside. "Here, let me teach you. This is how to punch."

"I know how to punch." Xena punched him in the leg.

"That's a sissy punch, Kid. You want a punch like this." J.R. took a stance and gave the heavy bag a punch that sent it swinging almost to the ceiling. He had to catch it to keep it from smacking him in the face.

"Wow!" Xena's said, her eyes flashing gold in the light. "You're strong."

"You can do it too . . . with proper training. Stand like this with your legs apart." J.R. positioned her feet. "Now, put your hand like this." He demonstrated. "And bring it back." Xena followed his motions exactly. "Good. Good. Now, do it faster. Good. Faster. Good. Now, do ten of those. Can you count to ten?"

Xena counted while punching the air. When she was finished the ten, he told her to turn around and punch ten times with her left hand. When she finished, he told her to punch with the right side again.

"My arms are hurting." Xena let her arms flop to the side.

"Means it's working," J.R. said.

Xena continued with two more sets before turning to him with her lip thrust out. "Can I stop now?"

"Sure."

"It hurts." Xena rubbed her arms. "Do you do that all the time?"

"Every day when I wake up."

Xena studied him. "Can I do it with you again tomorrow?"

"I thought you didn't like it," J.R. said.

"It hurts, but I get to play with you. I like to play with you. So, can I, please?" Xena clasped her hands and looked up at him with wide eyes. "Please?"

J.R. allowed himself a chuckle. "I'll get you tomorrow then."

"Yay!" Xena grinned so wide she squinted and hopped up and down. She then skipped out of the gym and up the stairs.

"The Kid's not so bad." J.R. said as he watched her leave. "And I found a way to relieve some of the extra energy she has." With one last punch to the heavy bag, he walked into to his workroom, and went back to work.

CHAPTER 17

"You have got to be kidding me!" Jané laughed as she looked at Celeste. "You spent $650,000 on that scrawny thing?"

Celeste clenched her teeth but said nothing. She was used to people talking about her like this. She was in Max's office at a place they called MFP. She didn't know what MFP stood for, but she gathered it was affiliated with the GFG Corporation's HQ somehow. The company's headquarters was a high rise building across town. It had sparkling windows and a sleek sign mounted at the top. Tess had shown her the building when she had brought Celeste here—she even pointed out Max's office at the top. But this complex was a massive single story building sprawling over a large piece of land next to the woods. Max seemed to prefer his office here. At least, that's what Celeste gathered. From what she saw, he had most of his stuff here.

Max was rifling through the papers on his mahogany desk. The office was painted white and had potted plants in the corner.

"I wouldn't exactly classify her as scrawny." Max opened one of his drawers. "Thin, maybe. But I think it's her body type."

Jané examined Celeste. Unconsciously, Celeste stood straight with her arms a little to the side to allow her to do so. "What are you going to use her for?"

"A new marketing campaign for the Freedom Project." Max

rifled through his files. "Where is it?" he muttered.

"Freedom Project?" Jané turned to Max. "Are we going forward with it? After the Jelu mess, I don't think the Board will go for it. And incidentally, do they know you spent more than half a million dollars on her? They'll never approve it."

"The amount I paid for her is not their concern." Max exhaled through his nose, tapped his fingers on his desk, before flipping through his drawers again. "But, yes, they know. And they approve."

"How'd you manage it?"

"Clever marketing." Max slammed his fist on his desk. "Where is it?" He sifted through his papers again.

"Um . . . what are you looking for?" Celeste said, her voice barely audible. She wanted to speak normally, but important people like Max and Jané intimidated her.

"My scheduler."

Celeste scanned the papers. Max's office was a mess. And she had thought him so meticulous when she had first met him. She spotted a flat tablet hidden underneath his desk calendar. "Is this it?" She pulled it out.

"Ah, yes!" Max took it from her. "Thank you."

"It's okay . . ." Celeste held her hands behind her back. "I'm a pretty good organizer."

"So, a new marketing campaign, huh?" Jané stepped in between Celeste and Max. Now, Celeste wasn't sure, but she thought Jané shot a glare at her. "What's she going to do?"

"She'll be the face of the Freedom Project. I've already set up photo shoots and interviews for her." Max gestured with his hands. "Imagine, even someone as closely guarded and expensive as the Pride of Terrance Claybourne's Prize Winning Collection has a chance at freedom! People will go nuts over it."

"That explains why the Board is on board." Jané chuckled at her terrible pun. Celeste didn't see what was so funny. Neither did Max apparently.

"The face of the Freedom Project, huh? Hmm . . ." Jané lifted Celeste's chin to examine her in the light. "It could work . . . with lots of make-up and wardrobe. She's kinda young looking."

"'Innocent' is the term I prefer," Max said. "People like innocent. It makes them want to protect them—makes them open their wallets."

"Not me." Jané turned to Celeste again. "Not for this mug anyway."

Celeste jerked her chin out of Jané's grasp. She narrowed her eyes before turning away from her. She did not like this panther one bit. And the conversation left a bad taste in her mouth. They were talking about her like property . . . like Terrance Claybourne did.

"What's the matter, rookie?" Jané smiled at her. "Freedom ain't all it's cracked up to be?"

"Yes . . . I mean, no. I mean . . ." Celeste trailed off.

"I know what you're thinking. You came all this way, and you're doing the exact thing you did when you were in slavery, right?"

Celeste gasped. That had been exactly what she was thinking.

"Reality doesn't always add up to our image of expectation." Jané shrugged. "But think of it this way: you're not doing this because you have to. You're doing this to earn your freedom. You have a choice. Once you pay Max back, you can leave and never come back here again."

Celeste gazed at Jané. Was she imagining things or did Jané's speech have a hostile undertone?

"Which reminds me." Max pulled a file out of his drawer. "Sign, Celeste." He set a piece of paper on his desk.

"You do know how to write, right?" Jané said.

Celeste responded by snatching a pen and writing her name on the line Max pointed to—the one right underneath his.

"The document you signed was an agreement." Max slipped it back into the file folder he had gotten it from. "You're agreeing to work until you pay off your debt. The rest of these are your papers including your Certificate of Freedom." He opened the folder so Celeste could see it. The certificate had blue lettering in the letter head and a gold embossed seal. "They're free and clear, but I'll keep it in here until you pay off your debt." He set the papers in a vault in the wall.

Celeste watched in dismay as he shut the vault on her freedom. "Why can't I get it now?"

"Because it's collateral," Max said, and when he saw Celeste cock her head continued, "Think of it like a car loan. I'm holding on to the title until you pay off your debt. But until then, you can do what you want with your freedom. You can even quit the company and go work for someone else for all I care . . . as long as you make payments on the debt. Once the debt is paid, you get the certificate. Simple."

"I see," Celeste watched Max twirl the lock for the vault. Her freedom would be safe enough in there. For now.

"Though it would be difficult to do your marketing campaign without her," Jané said.

"Good point." Max turned to Celeste. "Better stick with me, then." He winked at her.

Celeste felt her cheeks heat.

This time Celeste definitely caught Jané's glare. "Of course the real problem is: how are you going to pay back all the money." She leaned on Max's desk, blocking Celeste's view of him. "How long is this campaign going to run, Max?"

"Don't please." Max eased Jané off his desk. "I anticipate the excitement over her will die down in six months to a year."

"Not exactly a long time to pay it off." Jané fingered her chin. "What will she be doing after the campaign?"

"Not sure." Max leaned on his desk. "What are your skills, Celeste?"

"Um . . ." Skills? Celeste didn't think she had any. "I . . . I cleaned for Terrance . . ."

"We already have a janitorial team," Jané said. "They're excellent, and they don't need new people."

"I cooked." Celeste paused to think it over. "But I'm not very good."

Jané hissed in a breath through her teeth. "So not skilled, then."

"We can figure her out later." Max stood on his feet. "When the campaign is over she can take the skill assessment tests and such. Ready to go, Celeste?"

Celeste nodded and walked to the door.

"Max." Jané caught Max's arm to hold him back.

Celeste paused at the door to wait for him.

"You're going to lose a lot of money on this one, Max." Jané was whispering, but not well. Celeste could hear every word. "She's pretty much useless."

"She can be taught," Max said.

"She's sort of simple, though." Jané turned her eyes to Celeste.

"The amount of time and money it'll take to teach her won't be worth it."

Celeste clenched her teeth but said nothing.

"Maybe she can come clean my office while I figure out what to do with her." Max ran his hands over his hair.

"We don't need anyone else on our janitorial team—"

"She won't be on the janitorial team," Max interrupted. "I've yet to find someone to clean and organize my office the way I want it. And Celeste seems to get my system." He held up his scheduler as proof.

"What system?"

Max ignored her. "Even if she doesn't work out here, I have six months to figure it out other options."

"I hope you do, Max. I sincerely hope you do." Jané smiled at Celeste as Max joined her.

Celeste glared at Jané as she exited the office with Max. She'd show Jané what she was made of. She'd show her and anyone else who doubted her. Those papers would be hers one day. She wouldn't let anyone stop her.

CHAPTER 18

"What the CRAP!" Terrance slammed the holographic reader on the desk, cracking it. His whiskers twitched. On the screen, distorted because of the crack, was an article detailing the GFG's Corporation's Freedom Project—complete with an image of Celeste. The caption, "I made it out thanks to the GFG," was underneath her visage.

Terrance hissed at her and slammed his fist into her face. The reader sputtered and went dark.

"It's part of a new marketing strategy." FC frowned as he paced in front of Terrance's desk. "You wanted to know where Celeste went. There it is."

"This is Isha's fault." Terrance slammed his palm on the desk. "I knew something was funny when she said she had a family emergency the morning after Celeste got sick." He kicked the table. "I would have known something was up sooner if I hadn't seen Celeste go back to her quarters on the surveillance tape."

"That slave girl played you real good." FC shook his head. "You gotta do something, Terrance."

"Like what?"

"Isn't she yours?" FC's whiskers twitched. "Go get her back."

"According to the law, as long as someone pays the list price for the slave and gets the proper paperwork filed, she's free." Terrance yowled. "I can't fathom how they got their hands on her papers, and I didn't think anyone would pay over $650,000 for the wench!"

"Maximilian Descarté sure did, and he's ruining everything!" FC's tail bristled. "Their faces are all over the place . . . TV, magazines, newspapers . . . and this thing is gaining traction. Hundreds of slaves are running away, thinking if she can do it they can too. And the GFG is getting corporate sponsors . . . they're getting such good publicity over this, other companies want a piece of the action. He has to be stopped."

"Oh, he'll be stopped alright." Terrance narrowed his eyes. "I will personally ruin him and his company no matter how long it takes. And when I do nothing will spare that gray wench from my wrath. Nothing!"

CHAPTER 19

J.R. glared at his opponent standing across the meadow from him. She had her hands up to protect her face and stood on the balls of her feet. But her tail hung limp and relaxed—ready to offer her the balance she'd need in this fight. Just like he'd taught her.

In the years since he had taken her in, Xena had grown into a tall and lanky tweenager with no shape—but J.R. wasn't sure if it was because of age or body type. He almost hoped it was her body type. Less curves meant less boys he'd have to chase away from her, and he didn't think curves would suit her anyway. She wore her hair in a messy ponytail and shared J.R.'s disdain for frilly clothes and makeup and his love for sports and sparring. Which is what they were doing now. In fact, the only reason he was out here in this meadow was because their sparring lessons had become too rowdy for his basement gym. So he had brought her out here to where he met clients on those days he didn't feel like traveling too far from home. It even had a small hut across the grass for those times when being outside was a nuisance.

Kathra, on the other hand, had grown from a giggly, round baby to a laughing, round eight year old who loved sweets. She sat on the grass out of the way of the fray and held a digi-book in her hands—possibly some teen fashion magazine or a medical journal. Her golden hair had been caught back in a neat braid, and she wore a pink tank-top with a lacy, yellow, daisy-print skirt. Funny how she grew up so girly when J.R. was the one raising her. Maybe it was

Melody's influence.

"Ready for your beat down, old man?" Xena curled her hand into a fist.

"Watch your mouth, Kid." J.R. flexed his bicep. "I'm about to spank your little behind."

"Fighting banter." Kathra thrust her nose in the book, even though it was a holographic display of the text. "How droll."

"Droll?" Xena dropped her hands to look at her sister. "Kat, you read too much."

"And you don't read nearly enough." Kathra swiped the air to turn the page.

"Pipe down and count us in, would ya?" J.R. took to rocking on his toes.

"Fine," Kathra said, hiding a smile. J.R. suspected she secretly liked watching the show. "Three . . . two . . . one . . . Go!"

Xena darted at J.R. before the words were fully out of Kathra's mouth. She sprinted across the grass in less than the time it took for J.R. to swallow. But he was ready for her. He side-stepped her, and . . . uh, oh! She launched herself into the air at the last moment and corrected her aim to deliver a round house kick to his face. Man, she was quick.

Quick, but no experience. J.R. whipped his head out of the way, caught her foot, and swung her aside. She crashed into the ground and rolled to a halt, landing on her stomach.

Kathra burst into laughter. "What happened to teaching the old man a lesson?"

J.R. grinned. "Have to try a little harder than that, Kid."

"Ow." Xena pulled herself to her hands and knees. "That hurt!"

"Ah, stop wussin'. I didn't toss you hard." J.R. beckoned to her. "Shake it off, and let's go again."

Xena pulled her knees to her chest and hissed in a breath.

"She's really hurt, Mr. J.R." Kathra hopped to her feet.

J.R.'s ears pricked. "You alright, Kid?"

"I'm fine." Xena groaned as she stood. "I can't go again, though."

J.R.'s tail flopped. He *had* hurt her. The last time Xena quit on a sparring session, it was because she was getting a fever. He put a hand on her head to check. Nope, normal. "What's wrong, Kid? Tell me where hurts."

"I'm fine, really. I landed hard."

"Kid . . ." J.R. narrowed his eyes at her.

Xena bit her bottom lip, and her cheeks turned pink. "It's . . . that is . . . lately when I run around . . . my chest . . . hurts . . ."

"Your chest?"

"My chest." Xena gave him a look.

"Oh!" J.R. jerked his arm away as if she was contagious. "Yeah, well . . . maybe you should talk to Melody . . ."

"I did. She's taking me shopping this weekend."

"Good." J.R. sighed, glad he didn't have to take care of it. He shuddered at the thought of walking into *that* store.

"Shopping?" Kathra's tail fluffed out in anger. "Shopping isn't going to fix this! If Xena's having chest pains, she could be having a heart attack."

J.R. raised an eyebrow. "At twelve?"

"It could be a genetic condition. Or she could have angina or pericarditis! It's all here in the medical book I got from the library!" Kathra held up the flat, silver, holodisk player she had in her hands. "We have to take her to the hospital."

"Ugh!" Xena rolled her eyes. "Are you sure you're only eight?"

"My medical knowledge could save your life one day." Kathra grabbed her purse. "I know! I'll run a scan on her so I can tell the doctors what's wrong." She pulled out a purple and yellow scanner. She had gotten it for her birthday last year and wouldn't go anywhere without it.

"Relax, Kat." J.R. patted her head. "She doesn't have heart problems. She has puberty."

"But puberty doesn't cause chest pains. Unless . . ." Kathra's ears pricked. "Oh!"

"Yup. It's the beginning of the end for us." J.R. nodded gravely while winking at Kathra. "She'll be a teenager soon, which means she'll become all moody and irrational."

"She's moody and irrational already." Kathra turned her nose up. "What's going to change?"

"Shut up, you two!" Xena's face surged red. "Stop talking about me like I'm not here!"

"Relax, Kid. Geez!" J.R. swung around to face Xena with a smile of his face. "You're too easy to rile . . ." He trailed off. Xena's hair rose . . . . on strand at a time. He burst into laughter. "Kid, what's up with your hair?"

"Huh?" Xena patted her ponytail. "What's wrong?"

Kathra held her hand over her mouth as she giggled. "It's like you're touching a Van de Graaf generator!"

One of Xena's ears angled down. "A what?"

"A static electricity generator." J.R. touched the ends of her hair with a finger. "Your hair is all on end."

"Oh!" Xena jerked her head away from him. "It's my fur." She smoothed her hair down. "It's been generating a lot of static electricity lately."

"Maybe it the fabric softener you use." Kathra tried to get an angle on Xena to scan her. "They changed the formula recently."

"Stop scanning me, Kat." Xena hid behind J.R. "You're so annoying with that thing. I'm going to break it when you go to sleep tonight."

Kathra held it close to her chest. "You do, and I'll scratch your eyes out."

"Alright, alright. Enough." J.R. dug into his bag. "Since you're out of commission, Kid, I got something I want to test out on you."

"What is it?" Xena, with Kathra behind her, crowded around J.R.

He pulled out a small box. "Bioelectric communicators."

Xena put her hand on her hips. "Are you experimenting on me again, Mr. J.R.?"

"I might have something this time." J.R. handed her a small earpiece. "Doesn't have a large range, though. But you have to start somewhere."

"Your friend still working on this?" Xena stuck the earpiece in her ear. "It's been years—since I was a kid."

J.R. stopped himself from reminding her she was still a kid. "Research takes time. Shoving it in kinda far, ain't ya? I can barely see it."

"I have to, or it'll fall out," Xena said. "My ears are bigger than yours."

"Do I get one?" Kathra bounced up and down on her toes.

"I only got the one, but you can try it after me." J.R. put his earpiece in. "Okay, now all you have to do is think about transmitting a message to me."

Xena closed her eyes. "Can you hear me, Mr. J.R.?" Her voice rang in J.R.'s brain.

"No way!" J.R. swung around to Kathra. "Did you hear that?"

"No, what?" Kathra said.

"I heard her," J.R. said. "In my head."

"It worked?" Xena hopped up and down. "Send me a message."

J.R. closed his eyes. Can you hear me? he thought. But Xena said nothing. She didn't even flinch. "You didn't hear me?"

"No," Xena said.

"Blast!" J.R. stomped his foot. "Why are you the only one who can ever get these things to work?"

Xena rubbed the fur on her arm but said nothing.

"Can I try?" Kathra bounced on her toes.

"Sure." J.R. pulled the earpiece out of his ear.

Kathra stuck it in her ear and stared at Xena. She stared and stared and squeezed her eyes shut and groaned with the effort.

"I heard her!" Xena clapped her hands. "She said, 'Come on! Work!'"

"Yeah, but I think I said it out loud," Kathra said.

"I didn't hear you." J.R. stroked his chin. "Unless . . . Here, let me see it again, Kat."

Kathra handed him the earpiece.

After inserting it into his ear, he covered his mouth with his hands and said, "Kid, hop on one foot," in the tiniest whisper he could mutter.

"Why?" Xena put her hands on her hips.

"So you heard me?" J.R. tickled his whiskers. "So we have the same problem as before. The sensors aren't strong enough to pick up bioelectricity. Whispering might give it the boost it needs. But then, why can you use it?"

"Maybe I'm special?" Xena shrugged and forced a laugh.

"Oh, weird." Kathra stood with her scanner pointed at Xena. "The communicator is giving off this strange signal. Even when she's not using it."

"Stop scanning me, Kat!" Xena hid behind J.R. "You're so weird!"

"I am not!" Kathra stomped her foot. "Mr. J.R., tell her to stop calling me weird!"

"Even if he makes me stop, doesn't change the truth." Xena

stuck out her tongue at her sister.

"Mr. J.R.!" Kathra wailed in the high, whiney voice normally preceding tears. That voice grated at J.R.

"Enough, you two, I . . ." J.R. trailed off as his ear twitched. He was picking up something . . . the rumbling of an engine coming over the hill separating them from a dirt road. But who would come all the way out here?

"What's that?" Xena's ears swiveled in the direction of the rumble. "Sounds like a speeder." The rumble stopped.

"I'll find out." Kathra pointed her scanner at the hill. "Now, let's see . . . female . . . Genus: Canis . . ."

"Probably Melody." J.R. threw his towel around his shoulders.

"On a speeder?" Xena pointed out.

"Oh!" Kathra's ears stood straight up. "Species: Lupus, Subspecies: Lupus. It's a wolf!"

"But we don't know any female wolves," Xena said.

J.R. furrowed his brows. They didn't, but he did. Several, actually. But none who would want to visit him out here—if they knew where here was. None except . . . oh, crap!

"Stay!" J.R. said to the girls before he trotted over the hill.

A brown wolf, dressed in a red dress that showed more cleavage than fabric had draped herself over his speeder. J.R. shook his shoulders loose and ambled over. She fixed her violet eyes on him as he approached and smiled in a way that exposed all her fangs.

"Hello, J.R.," she said in a voice as smooth and luxurious as a finely distilled whisky. "Long time no see."

CHAPTER 20

"Vix." J.R. stood so that he was the only thing in her field of vision. "You're looking as . . ." He let his eyes run over her dress. It hugged her curves in all the right places. ". . . tantalizing as ever." His eyes examined every inch of her. She was in many respects J.R.'s ideal of beauty—slightly muscular arms and legs; long, shiny hair; pouty lips; curvy figure . . . though her chest seemed larger than her body type allowed. J.R. didn't recall that aspect about her. He would have remembered.

"I see I caught you in the middle of a workout." Vix ran the tips of her manicured fingers the wrong way up his bicep fur. "My, my. You're as cut as ever. Don't you ever age?"

J.R. rested his hand on the seat next to her. "I could say the same thing about you."

"You could, and you should." Vix tilted her head to the side, but J.R. stepped in to block her view. "Are you trying to hide something from me?"

"It's not a good time."

"What's the matter?" Vix's grin widened. "You got clients?"

"I'm entertaining two females over there, if you must know."

Her ears flattened. "Excuse me?"

"Jealous?"

Vix's laughter rang out among the shifting grass rustling in the spring breeze. "Not hardly! I wasn't the one who disappeared off the face of the planet after our breakup. Who knew you couldn't handle rejection?"

"Getting dumped by you doesn't bother me." J.R. shrugged. "Cause I know why you did it."

"Oh, do tell."

"You were starting to fall for me." J.R. leaned in close to her, letting his grin extend. "You couldn't handle it, so you got out. Simple."

Vix's grin faded into a frown. "You are so conceited."

"It's not conceit if it's true."

Vix rolled her eyes at him.

"So what are you doing here, Vix?"

"Can't a girl swing by an old flame to rekindle the magic?"

"I know you, Vix." J.R. crossed his arms. "The only reason you'd come all the way out to the sticks if you're in trouble or 'cause of money. Which is it?"

Vix pouted, her rose-tinted lips sparkling in the morning sunlight. But then she smiled. "Money."

"Thought so."

"I got a job for you, but . . . I haven't seen you around lately. I've been trying to find you for weeks now." Vix scrutinized him. "You didn't retire, did ya?"

"I've been around but nothing high-profile." J.R. sniffed. "Been taking easy jobs where I can get in and out, you know. Don't have time for anything else."

"Why not?"

"What about the job?" J.R. said.

"Fine, don't tell me. But I'll get it out of you eventually." Vix pulled a piece of paper from her purse. "The GFG Corporation is developing a brand new security device that will revolutionize the industry, and my client wants us to nab it." She held the paper out to him between two fingers.

"GFG, huh?" J.R. took the paper. "No wonder you need my help."

"Their security systems always kicks my tail." Vix tossed her hair. "I don't know how you do it."

"No stupid computer's gonna keep me out from where I want to go." J.R. read the contents of the job. "Terrance Claybourne's your client? What's he gonna do with a prototype security system?"

"Use it to keep in his collection? Sell it to the GFG's

competitors? How should I know?" Vix flicked the paper. "My only concern is getting the job done."

"He must be paying you a lot if you're willing to split it 50-50."

Vix sputtered. "50%? No, no! We'll split it 80-20."

J.R. raised an eyebrow.

"Okay . . . how 'bout 70-30?"

J.R. pressed his lips together.

Vix growled. "65-35, and that's my final offer!"

"Fine, but only 'cause you're so cute." J.R. flashed a toothy grin at her.

"You golden-tongued rogue, you." Vix tucked her hair behind her pointed ears. "So when should I—who is that?"

"Huh?" J.R. swung around.

Xena stood beside him, staring at Vix in wide-eyed awe. Her mouth hung open—"fit to catch flies" as his mother would say.

"Kid! What are you doing here?" J.R. tried to shove her back. "I told you to stay."

But she side-stepped him. "Wow!" She blinked as if clearing fog from her eyes. "You're beautiful!"

Vix started but then smiled. "Whoever she is, she's got good taste." She bent over to look Xena in the eye. "And what's your name, sweetheart?"

"Xena . . ." Her eyes wandered down to Vix's chest. They lingered there for a moment before turning to her own.

Vix chuckled. "Don't worry, cupcake." She patted Xena's head. "Yours will come in soon."

J.R. cleared his throat to interrupt. He didn't want Xena looking up to someone like Vix. "Alright, Kid. Back over—"

"Excuse me, Miss." Kathra squeezed beneath J.R.'s arm.

Vix took a step back. "Another one?"

"Not you too!" J.R. smacked his forehead. "Get back over there. Both of you!"

"But I want to ask her a question." Kathra opened her eyes wide. J.R. turned away—he'd learned not to make eye-contact when she was making that face.

"Let her ask, J.R.," Vix said.

J.R. shrugged. "Your funeral."

Vix bent over to Kathra. "What do you want, cutie pie?"

"How often would you say, on average, that you suffer from

backaches?" Kathra stood with a stylus poised over her scanner's screen.

Vix cocked her head. "I don't suffer from backaches."

Kathra studied her for a moment. "Impossible! You must be incapacitated most of the time!"

"What?" Vix turned to J.R.

"Don't ask me," J.R. said.

"According to my books, women with large . . . um . . ." Kathra paused to search for the right word. ". . . chests often suffer back pain because their back muscles can't handle the strain. And yours are . . . substantial."

"Excuse me?" Vix said.

"Enough, Kathra!" J.R. shoved her behind him.

"But Mr. J.R., I'm curious!" Kathra turned her big eyes to him. "It's your job as the adult to encourage and facilitate my quest to satisfy my scientific curiosity!"

"Take your scientific curiosity and get back over there! Pack your stuff, we're leaving." J.R. shoved her toward the hill. "You too, Kid."

"Aw, I never get to meet your friends even though you always have to meet mine," Xena grumbled. She caught Kathra's hand and pulled her along.

"But I'm not done scanning her!" Kathra said, dragging her feet.

"Get outta here!" J.R. kicked the ground, sending grass flying. He watched them climb the hill. "Sorry 'bout them."

"So . . ." Vix raised an eyebrow at him. "You're entertaining two females, huh?"

"It wasn't a lie. Not my fault if you've got your head in the gutter."

"Where'd they come from?" Vix's ferocious grin returned. "Some girl finally cornered you and forced you to take 'em? You payin' child support and all that jazz?"

"Sure." J.R. held up the paper Vix had given him. "I'll give you a call, and let you know when we're gonna do this."

"Aren't you going to tell me where you got those brats?"

"You seem to have come to a conclusion already."

"It was a joke. Anyone can see they got no wolf blood in 'em."

"True."

"Then where'd you get them?"

"Somethings are better left unsaid."

Xena and Kathra appeared over the hill again with all their things. They loaded them onto J.R.'s speeder and got onto the platform.

"I'll give you a call." J.R. mounted his speeder.

"Wait a minute!" Vix caught the handle of his speeder. "You're not going to tell me?"

"Bye, Vix!" J.R. took off, knowing she'd let go before she got hurt.

"J.R.! Don't you leave me in the dark!" Vix sprinted after the speeder, but soon got left behind. But her voice carried over the open meadow. He heard her cursing him until he left her behind the horizon. "It's too easy with her."

"Wow! She can curse!" Xena's eyes widened as her ears fell. "I've never even heard some of those words before."

J.R. glanced at Xena as she watched where they had left Vix behind. He'd have to take the long way around to get home—in case Vix tried to follow him.

"Hah! My scan is done!" Kathra lowered her scanner. "I figured out why she doesn't suffer from backaches."

"Why?" Xena turned to her sister.

"My scans show extensive surgery in the chest region . . ." Kathra gave a mischievous grin. ". . . fairly recent."

Xena gasped. "They're fake?"

The two dissolved into giggles.

"Does it even matter that I'm here?" J.R. bellowed.

They clapped their mouths shut.

"Sorry, Mr. J.R." Xena hung her head, and Kathra concurred.

J.R. nodded. Finally he had the upper hand as the adult here. It was about time he got some respect. He . . . a snicker escaped him. The two girls looked up at him. No. No, he couldn't lose it. Not here. They would never . . . Another snicker jumped out of him followed by a chuckle. He burst into laughter. "No wonder she looked different from the last time I've seen her," he said between breaths. "I can't believe you scanned for that."

The two girls joined him in laughter.

"You're getting too good with this scanner, Kitten." J.R. smiled at her over his shoulder. "But no more of that sort of talk, alright?"

"Okay," Kathra said.

"Now. I'm starving." J.R. swung his speeder in a wide curve home. "Isn't it about time to eat?"

"I'll make lunch as soon as we get in," Xena said.

"You know, every once in a while you remind me why I keep ya around, Kid."

"Because you love me?" Xena said.

"That too," J.R. said.

CHAPTER 21

"She's an attractive one, that's for sure." Jordan gazed at a poster of Celeste hung in one of MFP's hallways through the window of his office. "No wonder Max is so taken with her."

"It's the make-up." Jané stood beside him, crossing her arms and snorting breathes through her nose. "She's real homely otherwise. And Max is not taken with her."

"Then why does he let her hang around him all the time?"

"She's useful to him. You know Max. Once she's done being useful, he'll forget all about her." Jané clenched her teeth so hard they squeaked. "Though it is taking a lot longer than I thought it would."

"Jealous?"

"O-of course not!" Jané swung her face away from Jordan. "But I can't stand the little tart."

"Why?"

"She's too perfect!" Jané clopped her heel on the tile floor. "She always seems to have Max or Tess by her side, and they seem to be completely under her spell. And whenever she messes up, she bats her eyes and everyone goes limp."

"I haven't seen anything like that."

"She's got you too." Jané swung him around to face her. "Don't forget what your real goal is." She gripped his shoulder. "Don't you want to take over this complex? To be as rich and powerful as Max is? She could get in the way. I see it on the horizon."

"You're worrying too much." Jordan pulled her hand off his shoulder. "I have it on good authority Celeste's days are numbered. All her photo sessions and interviews are over with, and Max can't figure out what to do with her. Right now, he's got her running errands for him."

"She *is* pretty useless."

"But here's the thing: even though Max paid for her with his personal funds, he has her listed as a company asset. If he can't figure out a realistic way for her to pay off her debt, the company will make him get rid of her."

"So the letter I sent to the financial department made it." Jané let a smile come to her lips. "Sometimes I love those pain in the neck board members."

"But what will happen to me?" a small voice piped in.

Jordan and Jané swung around. Celeste stood in the middle of the hallway clutching a pile of papers to her chest. The office door was wide open.

"What the—" Jordan's fur stood on end. "What are you doing sneaking around here?"

"Are you spying on us?" Jané said.

"No! I was getting something for Max." Celeste held her papers out as proof. "You were the ones talking about me with the door open. Am I supposed to ignore people gossiping about me?"

Jordan marched over to her. "If you repeat anything you've heard, so help me . . ." He brandished a fist in her face.

Celeste gazed at the fist before smirking. "Why? What did you say?"

Jordan growled.

"Jordan, relax." Jané slid in between them. "Look, Celeste. There's a lot of things going on in this complex that less important employees aren't privy to. So if I find you're sneaking around leaking classified info to anyone—"

"I wasn't sneaking. I was walking."

"Fine, then." Jané turned to go back into the office. "I'll let it go this time."

"But what's going to happen if Max doesn't find a place for me?"

Jané turned and put on a sympathetic smile. "It's a bit difficult to say, but most likely, he'll have to get rid of you—sell your papers to recoup his losses. After that, whoever has the money to pay off your delinquent debt can acquire you. Maybe even Terrance Claybourne. I hear he's been trying to get Max to sell you back to him."

"B-but he can't. M-Max signed the paper too, right? It's like a contract."

"Here's the thing, Celeste." Jané put a hand on her shoulder. "Usually the Freedom Project runs more smoothly than this. We normally find a place for you before we make an investment. But you were an impulse buy. Max has to get his money back somehow."

Celeste's ears fell, and all her fur rose. "I-I can't go back to Terrance Claybourne."

"You best move may be to go to a different company to get a better paying job." Jané tapped her chin. "Oh, but, wait. You don't have any skills, do you?"

"W-what am I going to do?" Celeste started to tremble.

"Maybe you can talk to Max about it." Jané walked away from her. "But I'm not sure what good it would do."

Jané heard Celeste scurry away. She smirked.

"You are good," Jordan said. "And bad."

"Thank you, thank you."

"Do you think she heard anything incriminating?"

"She wouldn't have interrupted us if she had." Jané glared in the direction Celeste went. "But we need to keep an eye on her until she's out of here."

"I don't like the way she was able to sneak up on us like that." Jordan shuddered. "Creepy."

"But if you're right, she won't be around for much longer," Jané said. "We just have to make sure Max gets rid of her."

"Right," Jordan said.

CHAPTER 22

Celeste clutched Max's papers to her chest as she scurried down the hall to his office. Max was going to sell her? No way! She'd done everything he'd asked of her—ran his errands, cleaned his office, become the new face of the Freedom Project . . . she'd even ventured to remind him of things he wanted to do and meetings he wanted to schedule. He couldn't get rid of her now, could he? She slowed to a stop right outside his office. Maybe he could. After all, he had her papers as . . . collateral, she thought the term was. And if she didn't make enough payments on her debt . . . she bit her lips together. In order to stay, she had to do something to become invaluable to him. But what?

She took a deep breath as she opened his office door. She had to play it cool. Something would come up. It had to. "I have your papers, Max." She stepped in. The office was empty. "Max?" He must have left.

Celeste sighed. Max was always sending her for things and then disappearing by the time she came back. He never confided anything in her. And why would he? She was a slave-girl. Even the papers in her hands were sealed and classified. Not for her eyes. She gazed at the vault holding her Freedom Papers. When she was free—really free—then people would confide in her. Then she'd be important.

But until then, she had a job to do—as insignificant as it was. She set his papers on his desk, then organized and polished it, glancing at his desk calendar as she worked. Oh, dear! It seemed he forgot to update the time of his next meeting. It got changed from 8:00 to 7:00. Max always remembered those changes eventually, but usually at the last minute with lots of scrambling and fussing. He liked to be on time to things—early, even. She hated seeing him so rushed.

With a glance at the door, she uncapped a pen and marked the change on his calendar—as close to his handwriting as she could. As she put the pen back in its place, she sighed. She didn't want to leave this place even if she didn't have to go back to Terrance. It had become like home to her—she knew everyone, and she was safe here. What was she going to do if Max made her leave?

". . . You saved my tail, buddy." Max walked into his office, talking on his phone. "Thanks a mill. And did you happen to take a look at the communicator schematics? . . . I know you're no expert, but you do use a variety of devices in your . . . ahem, line of work, so I figured you'd know someone who—. . . uh, huh. Yeah, it's the problem I keep having. Bioelectricity is not strong enough to power it, but my scientists say is possible . . . Any ideas? . . . Alright. Well, keep brainstorming, will you? Talk to you."

Celeste watched Max dump the contents of his briefcase onto the desk. Papers spilled out everywhere. Another thing she'd have to organize later. She shook her head. He wanted everything in place, but never found the time to put them there. Well, putting them there was her job . . . for now.

"M-Max, can I talk to you?"

"In a minute." Max flopped in his chair. "First call Tess and get me some coffee. It's going to be a long day."

"Okay." Celeste walked out and used his secretary's phone to call Tess. Come to think of it, she hadn't seen Max's secretary in a long time. Maybe she got fired. And if she could be let go, there wasn't much hope for Celeste. She gulped, fixed Max his coffee, and returned to him.

He had his nose in papers when she set it on his desk.

Max picked up the coffee without looking up and heaved a sigh as he took a sip. "Okay, Celeste. What do you want to talk about?"

"Oh, um . . ." Celeste took a deep breath. "Are you going to get rid of me, Max?"

Max set his mug on the desk. "Why would I do that?"

Celeste set it on a coaster. "My interviews are over, and I'm not sure what my job is. And I know you spent a lot of money to buy my freedom. I heard if I can't work off my debt fast enough, the company will make you get rid of me."

"Who told you that?"

"No one in particular." Celeste shrugged. "It's a rumor I heard."

Max narrowed his eyes at her. "If you're trying to justify me keeping you around, lying to me is not the way to do it."

Celeste started. Her ears lowered. "Jordan and Jané. I heard them talking."

"Ah." Max leaned back in his chair. "They're half right. I am having trouble figuring out what to do with you. The skill tests we ran didn't reveal anything useful, and yet . . ." He trailed off, playing with his whiskers.

Celeste hung her head. So she was on her way out.

"But don't worry, Celeste. No one's going to make me get rid of you." Max picked up his papers again. "If I let them do that, I'd have to admit I was wrong. And I make it a habit never to admit I'm wrong. If I get rid of you, it will be because you can't hack it."

"So . . . there is a situation when you would get rid of me?"

"No one in this company is safe, Celeste. If they don't do their job properly, they won't have one." Max smiled at her. "All you have to do is do your job well."

But what is my job? Celeste wanted to say. But instead she nodded. "Yes, Max."

"Good."

"Yo, Max." Tess walked in, smiling at Celeste as she went. "Since when do you have her making your calls?"

"Since yesterday." Max went back to his papers. "I've been getting her to do new things—seeing how far she can go and how fast she can learn."

"So she's been running the office?"

"And keeping me on schedule to boot." Max turned his eyes to Celeste. "Don't think I haven't noticed your sad attempts at forging my handwriting."

Celeste flinched.

"Ah . . ." Tess grinned at Celeste. "Explains the terrible memos. Not much of a typist, are you?"

Celeste held her hands behind her back. "Never had a chance to learn."

"Hmmm . . ." Max stroked his chin. "Make a note, Celeste. You need typing and grammar lessons."

"Okay," Celeste said. "Oh, and did you call the board to set up the meeting you wanted to have with them?"

"Thanks for reminding me. Can you take care of it for me?"

"Yes, sir." Celeste darted out of the office and sat at the secretary's desk to make the note. So he had noticed her efforts, after all. This was fantastic! Now was the time to show him how useful she could be.

CHAPTER 23

 M ax watched Celeste walk out of his office. She had changed so much in the years since they had first met—the most notable being her hair. She had let it grow past her shoulders, a style that suited her more than her shorter hairdo. She also carried herself with more confidence, though she still wore those horrible, sacks she called clothes. They hung on her all wrong and did nothing for her shape. Honestly, she was going to have to do better if she was going to continue to work for him.

"So, Max, why'd you call me here?" Tess leaned against his desk.

"Don't please." Max gave Tess a gentle nudge.

"Sorry." Tess stood on her own feet.

"I found another copy—possibly the only other copy in existence. Had to pay a pretty penny for it."

Tess chuckled. "Imagine. A book of 'fairy tales' holds the key to unravelling the greatest scientific achievement in history! Bioelectrical components could revolutionize the way we do everything in this country."

"Besides our missing subject, that disk is the best source of information on cracking the code we can get our hands on." Max sat at his desk. "Expect your Research department to get real busy dissecting the data."

"I can't wait." Tess put her weight on one foot. "When are we expecting it?"

"Importing that particular disk was not entirely . . . legal." Max picked up a piece of paper from his desk. "So I made arrangements for it to be delivered to a place called Justin's Ridge."

"Never heard of it."

"Neither have I before this. It's not even on a map." Max laced his fingers together. "Perfect for our purposes. Needless to say, this stays between us."

"I'm offended you felt the need to say that." Tess exhaled through her nose. "So what's the plan? Want me to go pick it up?"

"After Squall, I don't trust anyone else to get it."

"It's been years, Max. Let it go."

"The last copy was lost because of him, and I spent seven years trying to locate another. I will not let it go."

"The disk being destroyed wasn't his fault. He didn't demolish the whole town, Max."

Max waved his hand to dismiss the topic. "We need a reason to go so I'm opening a computer store. I already have a location. Take the usual team. Once it's set up, I'll come by and collect my disk. You have a month."

Tess chuckled. "I'm surprised the company hasn't shut down all your 'personal business investments' by now."

"I make enough overall profit to warrant it." Max shrugged. "Besides, they usually don't know what I've done until after it's over."

"Eventually, they'll insist on more oversight, Max."

"As long as they get their paychecks, bonuses, stock incentives, and options, they'll do no such thing." Max stretched. "I do everything possible to make sure everyone in this company is taken care of. It's essential to my future plans."

"I wonder if you'll be able to pull it off." Tess sighed. "Maximilian Descarté, the new Minister of Defense."

"Count on it." Max leaned back in his chair. "When the time is right, Ol' 'Lion Heart's' fatal accident will open the path for me. I just need the right person to help me."

"Not Jané? I thought that was the plan?"

"I don't like her attitude lately." Max pressed his lips together. "She seems to be sabotaging Celeste."

"She never did like Celeste. I think it's all the attention she gets." Tess smirked. "From you."

"What attention?" Max turned to Tess. "I'm trying to get her to pay off her debt. I don't give her any special attention . . . do I?"

"No more than necessary." Tess snickered. "It's all in Jané's head, Max. Don't worry about it. You're rather clueless when it comes to those type of matters, anyway."

"What type of matters?"

Tess only smiled and shook her head.

"Whatever." Max snorted through his nose. "What about you? What's your opinion of Celeste?"

Tess glanced at Celeste who was on the phone at Max's old secretary's desk. "She's a little naïve. Funny, though, when you get her out of her shell. Surprisingly insightful and witty. Can't hold her alcohol, though. I like hanging out with her."

"I meant as an employee."

"Oh, well . . . she's a quick learner, intelligent. A little quiet, though—which may or may not be a good thing. Inquisitive and personable. Organized. Adaptable . . . why?"

"I'm thinking of promoting her to be my personal assistant."

Tess tilted her head in thought. "I can see that. She's trying everything she can to make your life easier. Plus, ever since she was set to clean your office, you haven't been yelling as much."

Max narrowed his eyes. "I don't yell."

Tess gave him a look.

"Much."

"Why'd you wait so long to consider her?" Tess turned to look at Celeste again. "It's been seven years."

"Has it been that long?" Max fingered his whiskers. "It's . . . because I was waiting for her to take some initiative."

"Or maybe you forgot she was around until you got the letter from the company's Chief Financial Officer." Tess stared at the ceiling a moment. "Why do you have her listed as a company asset, anyway? You used your own money to buy her freedom, right?"

"I couldn't enroll her into the Freedom Project otherwise. So I listed it as a loan I made to the company. They have to pay me back."

"You need to stop being so loosey-goosey with converting your personal assets to the company and vice-versa. The tax man won't like it."

"I reconcile everything with my accountants at the end the year. It's fine."

"You're going to get caught."

"Nah." Max smiled at her. "I'm too smart to get caught."

"If you say so. But it does make sense you would overlook Celeste for so long." Tess smirked at him. "You tend to forget about people you can't make use of."

"That's not true! It's . . . she blends in too much." Max threw himself back in his chair. "Half the time I forget she's in the room."

"Until you have to use her."

Max's whisker twitched. Tess knew him too well for his liking. "Shut up, Tess."

"The meeting is in an hour." Celeste peeked in through the office door. "I hope it's okay. It's the earliest time they were all available."

"It's fine." Max stood. "Come with me. We have a lot to cover before we leave for the meeting."

Celeste let her ears stand straight. "We?"

"Do me a favor after work, Tess." Max headed to the door. "Go with Celeste in town and get her some appropriate clothes." He stopped in front of Celeste. "I require everyone, male or female, to dress appropriately when they work with me. And those potato sacks you've been wearing won't cut it anymore."

Celeste's ears angled back a bit. "Oh . . . okay . . ."

"And make sure you get her some heels, Tess" Max said.

"Why?" Tess raised her eyebrow. "Are heels a requirement now?"

"I like women in heels. It's more feminine."

Tess scowled at him. "*I* don't wear heels."

"But you're not the feminine type. I've always seen you as more of the . . ."

"Oh, you better watch yourself, Max." Tess put her hands on her hips. "Don't say something you're going to regret."

Max pinched his mouth closed. He tried another tactic. "I think heels will look good on Celeste. She has the legs for it."

"Ugh! You're such a guy." Tess shoved passed him on her way out of the office.

"What's your problem?" Max called after Tess. "I'm just stating a fact about her."

Tess made a gesture that made Max's ears stand on end. "And you wonder why I don't consider you feminine," he muttered. "Let's go, Celeste." He strode toward the people mover that would take him over to his offices at HQ.

Celeste followed him without a sound.

CHAPTER 24

"What kind of business do you do again?" Xena stood at the door to J.R.'s bedroom with her arms crossed like some kind of cop.

"Don't worry about it." J.R. stuffed a shirt into his duffel bag. At least she wasn't trying to be cute. A cop attitude he could handle, but if she tried to be cute . . . he still hadn't come up with a secure defense against it.

Xena gave a growling grunt before she stepped in and pulled out his shirt. "Is this even clean?" She held it up in front of her.

"Dunno." J.R. tossed a pair of pants on the bed. "They were in my drawer." No use trying to pack now that the Kid was involved. She'd pull them all out to fold them.

She took a tentative sniff of the shirt. "Ugh!" She jerked it away from her nose. "It's filthy!"

"You put it in my drawer."

"Because you toss your clean clothes in with your dirty clothes after I do laundry." Xena tossed the shirt over her shoulder. It landed in the hamper she had bought for him. To date, he'd never used it. "I'm not your mom, you know. I shouldn't have to do this. You're supposed to be the adult around here." She fished a clean shirt out of his drawer.

"So you say." J.R. stuffed in a box of "working tools" in the duffel bag when Xena wasn't looking. "No one's asking you to keep house, you know."

"If I didn't do it, we'd live in a pig sty." Xena folded his shirt and set it in his bag. "Besides, who else is going to take care of you?"

J.R. tussled her hair.

"Stop!" Xena shoved his hand off, though her mouth was set in a grin. "So, when are you going to come back?"

"Three weeks ought to do it." J.R. glanced around the room to see if he needed anything else. "Every night, you go to Mr. Withers' house and sleep there."

Xena folded the pants he had tossed on the bed. "But we can stay by ourselves—"

"It's not a discussion."

"But—"

"Xena . . ." J.R. stared at her with his mouth set. His voice took on a tone Mr. Withers had used on him when he was younger.

"Fine." Xena stuffed the folded pants into the pack.

J.R. smiled at himself. Not bad. He was finally getting a handle on how to discipline the Kid. "Before I forget, there's a new store down the street from Mr. Deals' store."

"I can't wait to go in it," Xena said, lifting her head. "All the newest holo-disks are in there. I hope Mr. Deals doesn't go out of business 'cause that place looks so cool!"

"You're not allowed in," J.R. said.

"Why not?"

"Because I said so," J.R. said, "I don't want you near it, got it? Tell your little friends too."

"Right, right." Xena sat on J.R.'s bed.

"You need money for anything?" J.R. set his shoes on his bed.

"You're putting your shoes on the bed? Think of what you step in!" Xena slipped the shoes into a plastic bag before shoving them into the pack. "There's no food in the house." She smirked. "Again."

J.R. tossed her his wallet. "Buy food. The rest is for emergencies only. Got it?"

"Okay! Sheesh!" Xena plopped on the bed. "It's not like you haven't gone away before."

Kathra walked in while Xena rifled through his wallet, counting the cash and sorting through the receipts and papers he had left.

Kathra walked over to J.R., slipped her arms around him, and buried her face in his clothes.

J.R. felt a lump rise in his throat. The moment Kathra heard he was leaving, her constant smile fled from her face. She wandered around looking like she was going to a funeral. J.R. rolled his eyes. She was so emotional. Still . . . "Xena, take fifty and you and Kat buy something for yourselves."

"You're feeling guilty about leaving us, aren't you?" Xena said.

J.R. cast a look in her direction. Without a reply, he closed his bag and walked out the front door. He detached the platform from his speeder in order for Xena and Kathra would be able to make use of it in his absence and stowed it at the side of the house. "Xena, take care of your sister, okay?"

Xena nodded.

J.R. pulled his keys out of his pocket. "While I'm gone, Kid, don't leave your sister to wander around town by herself. Stay together, even during the day."

"That's not fair!" Xena stomped the ground. "Me and the guys have a soccer game, and Kathra hates sitting out there. She always whines and complains."

"You don't ever want to do anything fun!" Kathra turned her nose up at Xena. "You're always running around and getting all dirty. Why can't you be a normal girl and get some makeup or clothes that aren't old and have holes in them."

J.R. rapped the two on their heads with his knuckles. "You two find things to do together or not at all. I don't want Kathra running around by herself while I'm gone, and that's it." He turned aside and muttered, "And I'm not exactly sure those friends of hers are the proper influence on her."

"Can't I use the communicators you made to keep in contact with her?" Xena said.

"I can't find one of them."

"I have it." Xena pulled the earpiece out of her ear.

"Wait, you still have it?" J.R. scratched his ear. "I was wondering where it went."

"Kathra can have the other one, so we can stay in contact. Please?" Xena clasped her hands.

J.R. turned away from her pleading face. "You can use the communicators, but I still want you to stay together."

"But it's not fair," Xena said.

"Tough."

Xena crossed her arms and mumbled something about pointy-eared, wolf dictators.

A loud pop rang through the air. Kathra screeched and covered her head, looking up at the sky for the culprit. J.R. swung around, searching for the cause. The porch lights flickered on, sparked, and then exploded—reverberating another pop through the air. The lights in the house flickered on and then went out.

"I don't believe it!" J.R. threw his hands in the air. "That's the fifth fuse I've replaced this week."

Xena caught the end of her ponytail. "Maybe we should get Mrs. Thethe to check the wiring."

"She's already checked it twice." J.R. snarled a string of expletives at the house and its wires.

"I'll take care of the fuse, Mr. J.R." Xena said, patting his arms to calm him. "You go on your business trip. Everything will be fine by the time you get back." She forced a smile which soon faded into a tight frown. Her ears fell as she glanced at the house.

J.R. took a moment to calm himself. After all, he was the adult. "Don't look so worried, Kid. I'm sure the house is safe. It's not the wiring."

She jerked her head around. "What do you think it is, then?" Her eyes widened as she waited for his answer.

"I don't know," J.R. said. "But have Mrs. Thethe come again. Make sure she checks everything."

Xena nodded.

"Thanks, Kid." J.R. ruffled her hair again before stooping to hug Kathra.

Kathra hooked her arms around him. "I don't want you to go."

Xena pried her away from him. "Don't be a crybaby, Kat. We have twenty-five dollars each to spend. I'll change the fuse, and then we can get groceries and spent it, okay?"

"Can I get a dress? I saw this dress in the store. It was so beautiful." Kathra's wiped her eyes. "Or better yet, I'll get the new book I saw in Mr. Deals' store yesterday."

"New book?" Xena rolled her eyes. "Big surprise. What's this one on? The anatomy of surgical implants?" She and Kathra giggled together.

"Kid, I told you to knock it off." J.R. said, barely holding back a smile at the running joke.

"If you must know, it's book all about the scientific explanation behind Silver Foxes." Kathra hopped and down. "It's like the stories you used to tell me."

"Silver Foxes?" Xena crossed her arms. "People spent money researching that?"

J.R. mounted his speeder. "My tax dollars hard at work. Then again, I don't pay taxes."

"It could happen," Kathra's eyes sparkled, making them look like sea-emeralds under store lights. "Wouldn't it be cool if Silver Foxes did exist? They could fly and use lightning and save the world from evil danger and—"

"Keep dreaming, Kat." Xena ruffled her hair.

J.R. smiled at them. They always made him smile. Time to go. He may not have the heart to go if he lingered any longer. "I'll call you later. Have fun." He pointed at Xena. "Remember what I told you."

Xena waved him off, pretending she didn't care. But she did. She'd take what he said to heart. She was a good girl despite her upbringing.

J.R. tugged one of her ears, smiled at Kathra, and then took off on his speeder.

CHAPTER 25

Celeste hummed as she set another skirt into the cute purple bag Tess had helped her pick out. She was going on a business trip. Her first business trip. With Max! She giggled as she picked up a blouse. Her blouse. One she had bought with her own money. To put in her own space—even if it was only a small dorm room in MFP's housing complex. There was only enough space here for a bed, dresser, and closet. But it was hers. As was all these clothes she had gotten. And she was packing her bags to go on her first business trip. Maybe she did have a place in the GFG after all.

She and Max were going to a little town for the Grand Opening of a computer store Max was investing in. Tess was already there. So was Jordan. And Jané. Celeste frowned at the thought of them then shrugged. She couldn't have everything her way.

Celeste picked up a sweater to reveal a file folder filled with papers. Her hum faded. She had been so excited about her first business trip, she had done all kinds of research—marketing, finance basics, a guide to hiring personnel . . . anything to help make this store the most profitable business the GFG ever had. But her research uncovered something disturbing. Max had opened stores like this before, and a vast majority of them failed. She couldn't fathom it. The more she dug into these failed store's records, the more she saw obvious mistakes and sloppy business practices that made the stores fail. What if this new store was one of them?

No, no. Celeste shook her head. Max was smart—a business man. A CEO. She was a stupid slave-girl with no marketable skills beyond her fur. He should know more about this than she did. With a grunt, she shoved her research into the bag and zipped it up.

A glance at the clock told her it was almost time to meet Max, so she hoisted her bag and darted out of the door. Her heels gave a light "pok-pok" as she rushed down the tiled hall. When she had first gotten them, she could barely walk. Now she could balance enough to run. Not bad for a stupid slave-girl with no marketable skills.

"There you are." Max met her at the door to his office.

"I'm not late." It was almost a question, but Celeste was sure she was on time.

"You're not." Max took her bag from her and led her to the elevator. "But I like to be early."

They rode the elevator down to the complex's parking garage. Max strode out as soon as the doors opened.

Celeste crept into the garage. The entire thing was made of cement, and yellow lights overhead banished the darkness in spots. But only barely. Between islands of light were pools of darkness. Hers and Max's footsteps echoed off the walls—his a booming "clop" and hers a light "pok."

"Keep up, Celeste." Max made his way to a cherry, red sports convertible parked in the center of the garage.

"Oh, wow!" The car seemed to give off a glow that expelled the dimness in the garage. "This car is gorgeous!"

"I paid entirely too much for it." Max ran his hands over its smooth paint. "But it was worth it."

"It has wheels!" Celeste stooped to examine the black tires. She had never seen them on a car before. "Real wheels."

"It's an antique." Max opened the trunk to toss in her luggage next to his. "Not as fast as hover-models. But, man, can you feel the engine's power surging into you through the steering wheel. Makes you feel alive." He shut the trunk, causing a "thunk" to echo across the garage. "Hop in."

Celeste got in.

"Seatbelt." Max slid into the driver's seat. "I drive fast."

Celeste strapped herself in.

"Here." Max handed her his phone. "Call Tess and let her know we're on the way."

Celeste dialed the number. It rang and rang until it went to voicemail. "She's not picking up."

"Aw, shoot! Forgot about the time difference." Max reversed out of his parking spot. "Don't worry about it, then."

"Um, Max." Celeste said, as he pulled onto the main road. "I was looking up directions to get to New Jelu, and the GPS says it will take two weeks to drive."

"So?"

"Aren't we supposed to be there tomorrow?"

"We're taking the high-speed transport tunnel."

"The what?"

"You've never been in one?"

Celeste shook her head.

"Hmm . . . do you have any allergies or medical sensitivities?"

"Not that I know of."

"You should be fine." Max settled back in his chair as he joined traffic on the highway. "This will be a brand new experience for you."

"This is already a new experience for me." Celeste gave him a smile that made her nose wrinkle.

"Glad you left Terrance, then?"

"I'd be glad I left Terrance even if I had to live in a sewer."

Max chuckled. "Sometimes you're funny, Celeste."

Celeste turned her face to hide the color that came to her cheeks. There was something about Max that was so . . . charming.

CHAPTER 26

"Nah, man. I got you, Sherd." J.R. leaned back in his chair located in his apartment in New Jelu. He used this place as an HQ of sorts when on a job. It wasn't a big place, with not much more than a couch, a chair, a bed, and a place to set up his computers—enough to be comfortable and to be packed up in a hurry if need be. All the windows were open, letting in the smog, dust, and traffic noise of the rebuilt city.

"It's cool, man." J.R. scratched his scalp. "I've been off the radar for a while, and he forgot himself is all. I'll straighten him out fer ya . . . right. Just be sure to bring it when I get there, 'kay? . . . See ya, bud." He hung up the phone, stretched, and sighed. It felt good to be back in the saddle.

His front door flew open.

"Ugh! It stinks in here." Vix waltzed in as if she owned the place. She wore form fitting jeans and a low cut gold, sparkly shirt.

"There's the lady." J.R. swung around to his computer. "Was wondering when you'd show up."

"And I was wondering when you'd get in town." Vix flopped herself on the couch. A cloud of dust erupted from the cushions. "What the—?" She waved her hands in front of her face.

"Haven't been here in a couple of years." J.R. tapped on his computer. "It'll air out."

"Explains the smell." Vix stood and dusted her butt off. "When do we get started on the job?"

"Next week, probably."

"But you told me on the phone you're ready to jump. What happened?"

"Gotta do my research. That's the difference between your average thief and J.R. Dunsworth." He tapped his forehead. "I got brains, baby."

"And a few other things." Vix sat on his armrest, letting her tail brushing against his arms.

"Which reminds me." J.R. turned to her. "We got to go to the Cave-In tomorrow night."

"Ugh!" Vix shivered. "I hate what the place has become. It's wallowing in low-lives that look at me as if I'm a piece of meat— and not in the way I like."

"So I've heard." J.R.'s ears angled back. "I've gotta get them back in line. They're like children when their parents have gone out of town."

"And you're good at dealing with children, aren't you?" Vix smirked at him.

J.R. ignored her.

"So what are we going there for?"

"I need encryption codes for the GFG's security cameras. Gotta pick them up from my buddy and pay him." J.R. leaned back in his chair. "If I play my cards right, we can waltz right into the GFG without the cameras picking up a thing."

"You really are the best, J.R."

"I know." J.R. cracked his knuckles. "Now the hard part: I have to find updated security schematics for the building."

"Got it covered." Vix pulled a disk from her thigh pocket. "Got it this morning." She popped it into the computer.

"Where'd you get this?"

"My client provided it."

"Then it's probably outdated." J.R. spun the holographic, 3-D image of the GFG's HQ in the air. "The GFG's got the most high-end security systems of anyone in the business, and they're always changing their security protocols. That's why it's so hard to get in."

"Then how do you know your friend's encryption codes will be any good?"

J.R. grinned at her. "I know."

"Sure, right."

J.R. closed the schematics. "I'll keep it anyway. It's a good base to start with. They can't have changed every, little thing yet. It'll take me a while to get the remaining data so rest your pretty, little head till tomorrow night."

"Any chance I can skip going on your little excursion?"

"You don't want to go out with me?" J.R. turned to her with a mock-pout. "Now you're hurting my feelings."

Vix studied his face a bit, her lips pressing together. "Fine. I'll go find something to do with myself until tomorrow."

"You're a peach, Vix."

Vix waved him off as she walked out of the door without another word.

CHAPTER 27

"Whoa!" Celeste rolled down her window to gape at the massive tunnel frowning down on Max's car.

A row of vehicles had lined up down the road leading to a gaping hole marked by orange lights on its perimeter. The road had split into twenty or so lanes, each one filled with cars slowly approaching the tunnel. People in black and white uniform milled around, directing traffic, answering questions through drivers' windows, and maintaining order. At the head of the line, cars would approach a rising barrier, wait for tunnel workers to set the orange light to green, and roll into the tunnel. Celeste couldn't see what happened to them after.

She gazed up at the top of the tunnel stretching into the air. "Is this the high-speed transport tunnel?"

"Um, hm." Max rolled down his window at a monitor set on a stand on the side of the road. "Let's see . . . female . . . fox . . ." He tapped these options on the screen. "How much do you weigh, Celeste?"

"Um . . . 113 lbs."

Max tapped in the option. After a whirring sound, two pills in protective foil popped out of the machine. "Take these." He placed them into her hand. "Need water?"

"No." Celeste popped them into her mouth and swallowed them. "What were those?"

"Sedatives." Max pulled the car forward as the line moved on. "The transport tunnel uses coils to accelerate us to supersonic speed for a prolonged period. I'm not sure how the coils does this, but the process of acceleration has . . . uncomfortable side effects. You'll sleep through the whole thing with those."

Celeste gazed ahead. Sure enough she saw the vehicles at the front of the line enter the tunnel. A series of lights shone on them before the car seemed to stretch and disappear. She gulped. Their car was quickly approaching the front of the line.

"Um . . . what about you?" She turned to Max. "Aren't you taking any sedatives?"

"I don't like to take anything that will put me under the control of someone else." Max drove the car onto a platform. Clamps locked the wheels in place, and the car moved forward of its own volition.

"Please do not turn off your car's engine," said a computerized voice through the radio. "Set your climate control system to 'recycle,' place your vehicle in neutral, and enjoy the ride."

Celeste used her fingers to clean out her ears. The voice sounded like it was coming from down a tunnel. And her vision darkened at the edges. Her chest tightened. What was going on?

"It's okay, Celeste." Max said, patting her hand. "You're feeling the sedatives now. Don't fight it. Just go to sleep."

"But . . . I . . ." Celeste turned her eyes to the tunnel. The yawning darkness looked like a big, black maw about to swallow her up.

"Relax." Max smiled at her. "I won't let anything happen to you."

Celeste turned to him. Max, his blue eyes shining in the light, gave her a point to focus on as sleep overtook her. She was out before the tunnel started to accelerate them.

CHAPTER 28

Max gulped down his stomach as the transport tunnel jerked him to a halt. Nausea washed over him as the platform his car was attached to automatically transported them to a parking garage that allowed passengers to recover. His head pounded as the car was lowered to the floor and came to a halt. His stomach heaved . . . but the discomfort was a small price to pay for shaving days off this trip.

He popped some anti-nausea pills and turned to Celeste. Her tongue lolled out of her mouth, and she panted as if she ran a marathon, though she was still asleep. Sleep mitigated, but didn't eliminate, the side-effects of high-speed transport. She'd wake up groggy and dizzy once the medicine wore off. But she wouldn't experience sensations nearly as bad as Max was at this moment.

But he was used to it. His business took him all over the world, and the transport was the best and fastest way to travel. He reclined his chair and closed his eyes until he felt well enough to drive.

In fifteen minutes, he pulled out of the "rest and recovery garage" and joined traffic on the road heading toward New Jelu and by extension, Justin's Ridge.

He reached his destination . . . a small town in the middle of nowhere . . . at nearly three in the morning. He parked in front of the computer store his contact had told him about vaguely wondering where his team had parked. It didn't take him long to find the key where it had been left for him, so he carried Celeste—still unconscious—inside. Still foggy from the transport, he only had a vague impression of meticulously set up displays and electronics as he passed through the bottom floor to the stairs.

The second floor housed an empty apartment with a bed, couch, kitchen, and bathroom. He laid Celeste on the bed then collapsed on the couch without taking off his clothes.

He was out before his head hit the couch cushions.

CHAPTER 29

New or Old, there was always a part of Jelu which belonged to criminals. In Old Jelu, the area was a back road in the middle of town—small, dark, and chaotic. A hole in the wall where anything went. The only problem was officials who kept trying to clean it out. That led to most of the charges levelled against J.R. as he tried to defend his territory.

But when the city fell, J.R. and some of his cohorts decided to officially carve out a place in the new city for themselves. It was a fight, but J.R. loved a good brawl, whatever its form. A little fist action, some bribery, and a lot of intimidation later, they had sliced out a little corner of New Jelu for themselves. A place where the cops didn't go and where muscle, money, and violence ruled. And at the heart of it was the Cave-In, a bar where criminals could congregate, make plans, and settle disputes amongst themselves.

"Ugh!" Vix shuddered as she approached the place. "I hate this place. I can never figure it out."

"You're fine as long as you're with me." J.R. bypassed the line of young posers curious to experience the roughest place in town. He grinned. They were going to see a show tonight.

"J.R.?" The bouncer, a heavy set mandrill, immediately lifted the red rope. It was his job to make sure the clueless didn't wander in here. "Long time no see. Here for pleasure, I see." He exposed his fang at Vix—his attempt at a smile.

Vix shuddered all the way down to her tail.

"I'm here for business, actually."

The bouncer hissed in a breath. "Don't leave the place a mess."

"Can't promise you that, but I won't kill anybody tonight." J.R. flashed a grin at him as he walked inside.

The place was a big open space with a bar at one end; tables, booths, and chairs on the perimeter; and an open space in the middle. In the wings on either end of the bar were pool tables. Men and women of all species crowded in on the space. Smoke filled the air, and drinks sparkled in glasses.

In a booth to the right sat a small gerbil. He quivered in the corner, glancing around him with quick, jerking movements. A single light shone down on him.

"Sherd." J.R. slid into the booth across from the gerbil. "What's happening, my man?"

Sherd glared at J.R.

"Ew. What a mug!" Vix slid in beside J.R.

Sherd fixed his black eyes on Vix. "What's she doing here?"

"Same question I want to ask." Vix threw herself back in the chair. "Why do I need to be here?"

"I'm working with her on the job." J.R. rested his arm on the table. "Do you have it?"

"It's all here." Sherd held up a small disk. He inserted it into a small, flat box on the table. A list of alphanumeric code appeared in the air before them.

"Perfect." J.R. popped the disk out of the player.

"Here's a case for it." Sherd handed him a box the size of his palm. "It will keep it from being read by other unauthorized personnel."

J.R. set the disk in. "Hold on to this, Vix."

Vix slid it into one of her pockets.

"Now, about payment." J.R. surveyed the crowd inside the building. "Is he here?"

"At the bar." Sherd pointed with his chin to a gorilla drinking a beer.

"I see him." J.R. rotated his arm to loosen it. "How bad did he get you?"

Sherd turned his face into the light, exposing his left cheek. A shaved patch of fur was starting to grow in, and in its wake was a scar trailing from his eye to the corner of his mouth.

"Oooo . . ." Vix leaned backward. "What happened to you?"

"Badof did." Sherd glared at the back of the gorilla's head.

"I'll take care of it." J.R. turned to Vix. "Move."

Vix slid out of the booth, allowing J.R. to get to his feet. He strode over to Badof and tapped him on the shoulder.

Badof turned. "J.R.!" He opened his arms in welcome. "Where have you been?"

"Here and there." J.R. shrugged.

"And what brings you here rather than there?"

"Funny you should ask." J.R. socked Badof in the jaw so hard he flew off his chair and collapsed to the floor.

Silence fell. The crowd of criminals quieted and cleared a space for J.R. and Badof. The gorilla pressed a hand to his cheek and glared at J.R. who shrugged.

With a growl, Badof rushed at J.R. He shoved J.R. into a wall so hard the lights overhead shook. Before J.R. could recover, Badof clocked him in the nose twice. Stars flashed in J.R.'s eyes, but he didn't let it show. J.R. kneed Badof in the stomach and followed it with two more punches to the jaw and an uppercut to the nose. Blood seeped from the corner of Badof's lip. Badof wiped his mouth before whipping out a knife from his coat pocket. He rushed at J.R. again.

J.R. sidestepped him, smacked the knife from his hand, and elbowed him in the teeth. He caught Badof's head in his hands, head butted him, and smashed Badof's face in the bar. The gorilla collapsed on his back. J.R. knelt beside him and punched his face until blood and spit started to fly.

Badof groaned on the floor where he lay.

"Here's the thing." J.R. picked up Badof by his collar. "You messed with my buddy, Sherd. Gave him a nasty scar. You don't do that, man. Not to my guys. I don't care if he was on your territory. Sherd can go wherever he wants as long as he ain't double-crossin' nobody. Was he double-crossin' you when you jumped him?"

Badof groaned and shook his head.

"Right." J.R. thrust Badof's head to the ground. "The only reason you ain't dead is 'cause Sherd decided to be merciful. Otherwise, I woulda come packing. You got it?"

Badof nodded.

J.R. surveyed all the people in the bar. "You all got that?"

Everyone murmured an accent.

"I know I haven't been 'round a lot, but don't take it for granted." J.R. narrowed his eyes. "You never know when I'll show up again." He beckoned to Sherd who scurried over. "Now, what'd ya got to say to my bud, Bad?"

"Sorry . . ." Badof groaned.

"And . . . ?"

Badof only gave a questioning groan.

"Thank you for not wanting me dead," J.R. said.

"Thank you," Badof said.

Sherd nodded. His shoulders relaxed.

"Great." J.R. grabbed Badof's shirt and hauled him to his feet. "No hard feelings, man. Had to lay down the law. You know how it is."

Badof stumbled on his feet but gave J.R. a nod.

"Someone get him taken care of before he passes out!" J.R. called into the crowd. Instantly, two of Badof's companions rushed forward to escort him out. "One more thing!" J.R. said to the crowd before they dispersed. J.R. pointed to the bar where Vix was sitting. "Vix is my girl. We ain't a thing anymore, but she's mine all the same." He narrowed his eyes at some of the larger guys in the room. "Don't make her feel uncomfortable here. Dig?"

The crowd at large nodded then went back to their previous activities.

J.R. beckoned to Vix before heading outside.

"I love watching you bring the smack down." Vix linked her arms with his.

"I know." J.R. flexed his free bicep. "Why else do you think I brought you here?"

"We're not getting back together."

J.R. raised his eyebrow. "Who said anything about that?"

CHAPTER 30

"Do we have to go to the grocery store?" Kathra spoke in a high-pitched whine that made Xena's fur rise.

"Yes, Kathra. We do." Xena said between her teeth. "We can't continue to eat junk food for every meal." She glanced at Kathra out of the corner of her eye. Kathra was leaning out of the hover-platform Xena was towing, trying to scan something on their way. "Sit down. You'll fall out."

"We don't eat junk food at every meal." Kathra flopped on her bottom in the platform. "Miss Melody fixes us breakfast and dinner. It's only lunch."

"I like cooking lunch." Xena turned to Kathra. "Don't you like my cooking?"

"It's good, but . . ." Kathra flopped on her back. "I want a chicken sandwich."

"I'll make it for you today."

"It's not the same."

"I know. It's better." Xena towed the platform toward a group of boys loitering in front of the grocery store. "Hi, guys. What's up?" She walked up, slapping their raised hands as she approached.

"Xena." Mike, a brown rabbit, shoved his way through the crowd toward her. "Do you know anything about the car parked in front of the new computer store?"

"No. Why?"

"'Cause it's awesome!" Tommy, a black ox, clenched his fists in his excitement. "A bright red Condor A2Z Sports model with a 15 cylinder engine, and . . ." He lowered his voice to a hoarse, awed whisper. "It's on wheels!"

"Whoa!" Xena let the platform handle fall from her grasp. "An antique! I've never seen a wheeled car before!"

"Let's go down to the store and check it out." Carlton, a gray and white cat, pushed up his glasses. "And we can check out the new video games there while we're at it."

"Mr. J.R. told us not to go there." Xena leaned on the wall to cross her arms. "He won't tell me why, though."

"*Mr.* J.R.?" Mike raised an eyebrow at her. "Don't tell me you still don't have the nerve to call him 'Dad.'"

"I've been working up to it." Xena kicked a pebble into the road.

"You've been working up to it for months now. Just do it." Tommy said.

"I will," Xena said.

"In any case, we don't have to go inside the store to check out the car, do we?" Thompson, a crane, ran a feathery finger down his beak.

"But I wanted to go in . . ." muttered Carlton.

"The car is cooler anyway. Let's go!" Tommy headed off followed by the rest of the guys.

"Awesome!" Xena trotted along with them.

"But Xena!" Kathra rushed over to her. "You can't. We're not allowed."

"We're not allowed." Tommy made his voice a high-pitched replica of Kathra's whiney voice. "Seriously? Baby sisters are so childish! Are you coming, Xena, or are you going to stay with the toddler."

"Don't talk about her that way." Xena turned her nose up at him but turned to Kathra. "Don't worry about it, Kathra," she said using her communicator. "It'll be fine."

"But, Xena—" Kathra whispered also using the communicator.

"If you don't want to come, wait here. I'll be right back." Xena jogged after the boys.

Kathra hesitated a moment before jogging to catch up with Xena.

"It'll be fine." Xena patted Kathra's head. Kathra gave a whimpering groan.

The car was parallel parked on the side of the road, its top down. The sun gleamed off the shimmers in the red paint and dazzled Xena's eyes.

"This is beautiful!" Xena ran her hands along the side. "It's metal."

"Cool!" Carlton leaned in over the door. He turned to Xena with a mischievous grin. "Dare you to get inside it."

"Are you kidding?" Xena took a step back. "I'm not stupid."

"That's debatable," Kathra said with the communicator.

Xena narrowed her eyes at her.

"What about you, Mike?" Tommy elbowed Thompson while glancing at Xena. "A stunt like that would impress anyone." He, Thompson, and Carlton stifled a snicker, though Xena didn't see what was so funny.

"Oh, please!" Xena rolled her eyes. "Mike would never do something like that. He wouldn't dare."

Mike's ears reddened a bit. "I can so! Watch me."

"Mike, what are you doing?" Xena watched as he shifted his weight to hop in. "Are you crazy? You're going to get us in trouble!"

"I'm no chicken!" Mike started to climb over the door.

"Don't be stupid! Get off!" Xena caught his elbow to pull him off. He tumbled backward, causing Xena to lose her balance. She caught the car door to keep upright.

"Hey, you kids! Get away from there!" A vixen appeared at the computer store entrance.

"Scatter!" Tommy sprinted down the road. The rest of the boys dispersed.

"Let's go, Kat!" Xena turned to run, but her shirt had snagged on a metal bur on the edge of car door. "Hey!" She yanked and yanked, but her shirt was stuck fast. It started to rip right at the waist.

Kathra hopped up and down. "Xena, come on!"

"I'm stuck!" Xena tried to unsnag her shirt. "Stupid metal cars!"

"I told you to get away from the car!" The vixen marched over to Xena. "Do I need to call the police?"

"I'd gladly go, but I'm stuck!" Xena motioned to her shirt.

The vixen examined her shirt. "Oh, you're right."

"Can you help me?" Xena gazed up at the vixen. She had cool gray fur, and black hair—like hers. But even though they were the same, this vixen was more graceful with her high heels, dress shirt, and flitting black skirt. Her hair slid over her shoulders, and her fur was brushed nicely. Even her green eyes sparkled in the sun. Xena had never met a vixen like her before.

"Hold still, I think I can . . ." The vixen took Xena's shirt in her hands, brushing against her arm in the process. A spark jumped between them. "Ouch!" The vixen hopped back. "You shocked me!"

"Sorry." Xena smoothed her fur down. "Static electricity. I get a lot of it this time of year."

"That's the strongest static shock I've ever felt." The vixen rubbed her shoulder. But after a moment, she took Xena's shirt again. She unhooked the snag, and Xena hopped free. "There, no harm done." The vixen ran her hand over the paint. "Though, I hope this nick was there before."

"It must have been. We didn't do it." Xena examined her shirt. There was a small hole where it had been snagged. "Me and my friends weren't trying to hurt your car. We've just never seen one like it before."

"It's not my car. It's my boss's. I don't know how to drive."

"Really?" Xena examined the vixen up and down. "I thought all adults drove."

"Not me." The vixen's eyes trained Xena up and down. Her ears angled back. "You know, I've never met another fox with gray fur before. And yours is beautiful. It's so shiny and silky, and it sparkles like silver."

"Silky? My fur?" Xena extended her arm so it caught the light. "No one's ever said anything like that to me. Do you really like it?"

"Absolutely." The vixen nodded. "It's lovely."

"Xena, come on!" Kathra pulled on Xena's arm. "We're not allowed."

"Fine." Xena smiled at the vixen. "Nice meeting you. Oh, what's your name?"

"Celeste."

"I'm Xena." Xena let Kathra pull her away. "Bye. Maybe I'll see you later."

"Bye." The vixen waved back.

"Wow! She was so cool." Xena watched Celeste over her shoulder as she went.

"We shouldn't have been over there." Kathra crossed her arms. "Mr. J.R. is going to be so mad at us if he finds out—"

"He's not going to find out as long as you don't say anything and I don't say anything, right?"

Kathra nodded.

"Good. And it's not like we did anything wrong. We didn't go in the store." Xena opened the door to the grocery. "So don't worry about it, okay?"

Kathra heaved a deep breath. "You're right. Just . . . don't go over there again."

"I won't," Xena said.

CHAPTER 31

"An adult, huh?" Celeste turned back to go inside the store. "I guess I am an adult. I never thought of myself that way before." She halted. "Oh, shoot! I should have asked her how she got her fur so shiny. Oh, well." She walked into the computer store.

Jané, Jordan, and Tess stood behind the counter. They all had nametags on as if they were manning the computer store.

"Got it all sorted?" Tess said.

"Yup." Celeste gazed at all the products displayed around the store. "Though it probably would have been better to invite those kids inside. Business doesn't seem to be going so well."

Everyone in the store chuckled.

"What's so funny?" Celeste looked around at everyone's face. "I'm serious. I don't even this this is a good place for a computer store in the first place. It won't be successful here, and . . ." She trailed off as the rest of them snickered. "Am I missing something?"

"Must be terrible to be out of the loop." Jané sat on the counter.

"Well, someone put me in the loop." Celeste clenched her fists. "This store is completely empty. What is Max thinking?"

"I thought my ears were unusually itchy." Max descended the stairs. He had a hand on his head, and his teeth were clenched. "Where did you go, Celeste?"

"Some kids were messing with your car, but I chased them off." Celeste approached him. "Are you okay? You look awful!"

"Headache," Max said through his teeth. "Side effect of the high speed transport."

"Then maybe next time you should take the sedatives," Tess said.

Max merely stiffened his whiskers at her.

Celeste bit her lips together. Someone had to say something about this. "Max, there's something I want to talk to you about."

"Go on."

"It's this store."

Jané snickered. "This should be good."

Celeste ignored her. "Opening this store was a mistake."

"Was it?" Max's mouth widened in a grin.

"The location is out in the middle of nowhere; people here aren't interested in these type of products; and there's another computer store down the street!" Celeste took a deep breath. "But that's not the worst of it."

Max leaned against the front counter. "Oh, and what is?"

"The GFG Corporation has a history of starting stores like this all over the country. Most of them never do well, and undergo bankruptcy within the year!" Celeste paused to take a deep breath. "You can't keep doing this, Max. And someone should have told you, but you've surrounded yourself with 'Yes Men' who won't tell you the truth!"

"Yes men?" Tess chuckled. "Me included?"

Celeste started. She hadn't meant to offend Tess.

"Who do you think you are?" Jané thrust her hands on her waist. "Calling us 'yes men'!"

Celeste flattened her ears. She didn't have a problem offending Jané. "Have you told him what a bad idea this was? Or do you secretly want Max to fail?"

"How'd you learn about all those stores, anyway?" Jordan said. "Spying?"

"It's public record," Celeste said.

"So." Max walked between her and the rest of his team. He had a smirk on his lips. "Do you think you're the one who will tell me the truth?"

"Well, yeah . . ." Celeste lowered her eyes. "You saved me,

Max. I want you and this company to do good . . . And if it means I say something you don't like sometimes, I will."

"Brown noser!" Jané sang. Celeste glared at her as the rest of the team laughed. Celeste didn't see what was so funny. She didn't have a brown nose. Hers was pink. And even if it was brown, what did it have to do with anything?

"If you want to help," Max said, his voice slicing through the tension, "go run an errand for me." He pulled a piece of paper from his back pocket. "Find this store and pick up this order."

"O-okay." Celeste backed toward the door. "But what about the store?"

Max's smile faded. "Just go get it, Celeste."

"Right. I'll be back." Celeste opened the door to leave.

"I can't stand her," Jané said as Celeste walked out the door. "I have never met a more simpering, pathetic creature. Why did you bring her here, Max? She's useless."

Celeste rushed down the street. She didn't want to hear Max's answer.

CHAPTER 32

"I have never met a more simpering, pathetic creature." Jané crossed her arms as Celeste trotted down the street. "Why did you bring her here, Max? She's useless."

"There's something about her I like." Max watched her scamper down the street until she was out of sight. "I'm trying to figure out what."

"Besides the fact she organizes your life?" Tess smirked at him.

Max didn't grace her with an answer.

"She's creepy." Jordan snorted through his nose. "She'll be around, and no one will know she's there. Then when you least expect it . . . bam! There she is!"

"I've noticed it too." Max stroked his chin. "It could be useful."

"No way!" Jordan growled. "She's a sneak. She might be a corporate spy or something."

"Oh, come on, Jordan." Tess rolled her eyes. "If she is a spy, I think we would have noticed something over the last seven years she's been working for us."

"I don't even know why we're wasting breath discussing her," Jané said. "She's a simpleton who's only good for running errands. While she's gone, let's get this thing done. We need to pick up the package, right? Where is it?"

"Celeste is getting it." Max massaged his temples. His head was still hurting. "It's where I sent her."

"But I thought you came all the way out here to you could pick up the package personally." Tess leaned on the counter. "You didn't trust anyone else to pick it up. Not even me."

"It's another experiment." Max shrugged. "I want to know if I can trust her."

"Even above the rest of your team?" Jané put a hand on her chest. "Above me?"

"Who I trust with what not your concern, Jané." Max clenched his teeth as his head throbbed. "You all do your jobs and let me worry about Celeste. Now if you'll excuse me, I'm going to find some headache medicine. Tess, if Celeste comes back before I return, call me."

"You got it, Boss," Tess said.

Max headed back up the stairs, knowing he'd made part of his team angry. But he couldn't concentrate on it now. All he could think about was getting some headache pills.

CHAPTER 33

Celeste trotted down the sidewalk, her ears flattening as she thought of everyone back at the store—especially Max. What was so funny about her wanting to help anyway? And why was everyone acting so strange? It felt like she was missing something. But, oh, well. She shrugged her cares off. What mattered now was doing what Max asked and proving she was an asset to him.

It didn't take long for Celeste to walk to the computer store Max wanted. The outside looked like every other store in this town with its faded awning and weathered wood. But this one had the cracked and faded words: "Deals' Computer Deals" printed on its awning.

Celeste shook her head at the name. Corny and a pun. Probably what passed as humor in a town like this. She walked inside, joined the line, and looked around.

The store was filled with computer equipment, cameras, tablets, phones, video games, and holo-equipment . . . a general electronics store. But all the gadgets were out of date. Interesting Max's store didn't attract more attention than it did.

The bell jingled, and the two fox kits she had met earlier walked in. The white one walked straight to the line while the gray one . . . Xena . . . spoke to some boys that came in with her.

"I don't care," she was saying. "You all left me behind to get in trouble. I would have stayed with you. You guys are the worst!"

Celeste smirked. Perhaps she was telling them about their encounter earlier.

"Next." A meerkat behind the counter looked at her with a nervous excitement. "Welcome to Deals' Deals. What can I do for you, young lady?"

"I have to pick up a shipment, please." Celeste held out the order form Max had given to her.

"Ah, yes!" Mr. Deals said after he looked at her order form. "I don't think I've ever had an order for 144,000 holo-disks before—each one in their own, little box. One moment. Let me get it for you."

"Thanks." Celeste watched him as he went to the back. Then she turned to the kits. The gray one had joined the white one in the line. "Hello again, Xena!"

The white fox stiffened, but the gray one's ears pricked.

"Oh, Miss Celeste!" she said.

"Fancy meeting you here."

"I know, right?" Xena chuckled. "It's like you're following me."

"Your fur is bound to attract attention." Celeste chuckled in turn. "I'm happy I bumped into you again. I wanted to ask you, how do you get your fur so shiny?"

"I don't know." Xena examined the fur on her arm. "It must be the shampoo we use. What's the name, Kat?"

"Silken Fur." Kathra hid behind Xena.

"She's the one who picks it out." Xena pointed at Kathra with her chin.

"I've never heard of it," said Celeste.

"It's a regional brand," Xena said. "You can get it at the grocery store down the street. Come to think of it, we need to go back there. I forgot the eggs. That's what I get for not making a list."

"And we have to hurry," Kathra said. "The ice-cream will melt."

Xena groaned. "If only we didn't have to walk down that long road through the forest. It's like all those trees trap in the heat. We'll have ice-cream soup by the time we get back."

"Here we go!" Mr. Deals returned with a largish box in his hands. "144,000 holo-disks—each in its own packaging."

He handed Celeste a box with clear tape on the top and brown tape on the bottom. "Was this box opened?" she asked.

"I check all shipments coming through here." Mr. Deals said tipping an imaginary hat. "In this case, I found a book in with all the other blank holo-disks. So I replaced it. If you have any problems you can bring it back within 30 days, and I'll replace it."

"Thank you." Celeste hoisted the box.

"A book? The one you told Kat about?" Xena approached the counter as Celeste headed to the door.

"Yup!" Mr. Deals said. "I couldn't get a hold of anyone to return it to, so . . .you need help with the box, miss?" he said to Celeste.

"I got it," Celeste said, walking to the door. "Thank you!" She hefted the box to get a better grip on it as she walked down the sidewalk. "I wonder why Max needs this many disks. You'd think a computer store would have enough. Another bad financial decision." She sighed. "Then again, Max is smart, and so is Tess." She growled in her throat. "Even Jané and Jordan know what they're doing. Maybe I am making a fool of myself. Maybe I should shut up and go with the flow." With lowered ears she walked back into her computer store.

"That was quick," Max said as she walked into the store.

"The town is not that big," Celeste said, a bit bitterer than she meant it.

"Celeste, you sound salty today," Tess said.

"Probably can't stand this small town life. Neither can I." Max took the box from her. "Let's go, Celeste."

"We're leaving?" Celeste trotted to open the door for him.

"This is all we came here for." Max walked outside.

"Don't tell me *that's* the whole reason we opened this store?" Celeste gaped at him then the others. "Couldn't you have gotten it delivered?"

"Careful, Celeste. Your idiocy is showing." Jané stood with her hands on her waist. "Max, are you sure you want to let her in on this?"

"I'll decide what I let her in on, thank you, Jané." Max said, but he glared at Celeste. "Let's go."

Celeste took one last look at everyone before she joined him.

"Jané, does have a point, Celeste." Max stowed the box in the trunk. "You're getting a nasty habit of asking questions. If you want to get far in my company, stop it."

"But how am I supposed to learn if I don't ask questions?" Celeste said, getting into the car.

"Keep your eyes open." Max got in the driver's seat. "From what I've seen, you're good at that."

Celeste started. She didn't remember Max ever directly complimenting her before.

"Celeste, are you shedding?" Max swatted the fur on his arms. "Your fur is everywhere!"

"No." Celeste turned to Max and caught sight of a gleaming sliver of thread. She picked it up. It was a strand of shimmering, gray fur. "It's not mine. It must belong to that girl. She was one of them I had to chase from your car. Her fur was so shiny." She placed her hands on her cheeks.

"Did she get inside the car? No, wait . . . it's stuck on the outside of my car door." Max pulled a strand of fur from the door. "What the—this fur is . . . it's shining!"

"I know, right! You should see it on her. I've never seen fur so beautiful. It was probably people with fur like hers that started the myth about Silver Foxes. If you saw her, you would almost think they really existed."

Max gave her a look. "Silver Foxes?" Celeste nodded, and every strand of fur on his body rose. "Tess! Tess!" He vaulted out of the car and sprinted into the store.

"M-Max?" Celeste looked after him. He rushed in and spoke to Tess with arms flailing. In a few moments, Tess walked out. She glanced over her shoulder at him, one eyebrow raised.

"What fur is he talking about, Celeste?" Tess asked as she approached.

"Um . . ." Celeste gathered a few of the pieces of fur from the nick Xena had been caught on. "Here. What's going on?"

Tess took the fur strands. "It's nothing you need to worry about." She pulled a mobile scanner from her back pocket and scanned it. Celeste didn't know much about scanners, but she knew this one had a built in computer to interpret results. "What the—" Her eyes widened as she read the results.

"I'm telling you, it's nothing." Max walked out with Jané and Jordan behind him. "What's the verdict, Tess?"

Tess turned to him. "Max, there is four times the amount of metal in this fur than usual."

Celeste leaned toward Tess. "Is it dangerous?"

"The girl you met, Celeste." Max pushed passed Tess before she could answer. "How old was she?"

"Um . . . I'd say 11 . . . maybe 12."

Max turned to Tess who grinned. "Five plus seven equals twelve," she said.

"This town is better than I expected," Max said, rubbing his hands together.

Jané thrust in between them. "Why are we getting so excited about a math problem?"

"Never mind." Max leaned close to Celeste. "Where did she go?"

"She said she needed to go to the grocery store. She forgot eggs or something."

"Perfect." Max hopped in the car. "Pack up, and get ready to go. I want to leave as soon as I give the word. Leave Pete to take care of the store. Tess, get ready."

Tess grinned wide. "Yes, sir."

"Jordan, you come with me." Max grinned as he put his hands on the steering wheel. "May need your help with an extraction."

Jordan chuckled as he jumped in the back seat.

Max started the car and took off as Jané complained about the lack of information. His grin widened as he went.

"Max, why are you looking for this girl?" Celeste asked as she watched the stores whizz by. "What do you want with her?"

Max's grin faded into a frown. "Celeste, what did I tell you about asking questions?"

"Sorry." Celeste clapped her mouth shut. She didn't dare to make another noise throughout the car ride to the grocery store.

CHAPTER 34

Max screeched to a halt in front of the grocery store and hopped out of the car. Jordan followed him without a word.

Celeste sighed as she got out of the car.

Max burst into the store. He glanced one way then the other. "Jordan, split up. Looking for a girl with gray fur."

Jordan grunted an assent and the two of them took opposite sides of the store and searched aisle by aisle. Celeste remained at the front door, shaking her head in bewilderment.

"What in tarnation's gotten into them?" asked a dog behind the counter. Her nametag read Melody.

"I have no idea." Celeste walked to the counter to speak with her. "I think he's looking for a girl I spoke to earlier. She has beautiful silver fur. Do you know her?"

Melody narrowed her eyes. "Why are you looking for her?"

"It must have something to do with Max's car," Celeste said, even though she was more than 70% sure it had nothing to do with it. "She was hanging around it earlier, and I noticed a little nick on it after. I'm sure it's nothing, but Max is fussy about everything."

"I thought J.R. told them not to go around there." Melody bit her lips together. "Are they in some sort of trouble? They live on the edge of town. I can call them over if you need to speak with them. But if there was any damage, I'll pay for it right now."

"Did you find her?" Max met Jordan in the middle aisle.

Jordan shook his head. "What's so special about her anyway?"

Max didn't answer. Instead he marched over to the counter. "Hey, you girl," he said to Melody. "You work here?"

Melody studied Max up and down. Her ears angled back as she did. "I do. May I help you, sir?"

"I'm looking for a girl—gray fur, black hair." Max clenched his teeth. "Seen her?"

Melody let her eyes drift over to Celeste. Her brows rose.

"Not her." Max stiffened his whiskers. "The one I'm looking for is a child."

Melody inhaled through her nose as if making a decision. "Look. I heard about your car."

"My car?" Max's ears flattened.

"If she did any damage, I'll pay for it." Melody opened the register. "Just tell me how much."

"I'd rather take care of the problem myself." Max crossed his arms. "Her address."

"I'd rather not give it out." Melody picked up the phone. "But I can call her to discuss—"

"You will do no such thing, Melody." An old dog hobbled over to them. He had a slight limp but was otherwise hale and healthy. He looked like the type of old, stern, yet loving grandpa Celeste wished she had. She couldn't help but smile at him. "Listen here, young pup. I know Xena, the young girl you're accusing of damaging your car, and she wouldn't do any such fool thing."

"I never said she damaged it," Celeste said.

But the old dog went on heedless. "Even if she did do it, my daughter done said she'd pay for it. So take your money and go!"

"Stay out of this old man." Max's voice dropped to a growl. "This isn't your business."

"Everything going on in this town is my business, pup!"

"I'm saying it isn't." Max turned to the dog. Jordan loomed behind him and crossed his arms, making his muscles bulge.

"You think I'm afraid of you?" The old dog stood to his full height. "Why in my day I've faced down guns and . . ."

Max rolled his eyes as the dog continued. "This is why I hate old people." He pulled his gun from his coat and shot the dog in the leg.

Celeste hopped back as the old dog dropped to the floor and

clutched the wound.

"Dad!" Melody rushed to his side. "Leave him alone!"

"Next shot is fatal." Max pointed his gun to the dog's head. "Where is the girl?"

"Don't tell them nothing, Melody," said the dog through clenched teeth.

But even if he hadn't said it, Celeste didn't think Melody would reveal anything. The look in her eyes said it all. Celeste knew her type—tough and hardened yet soft and caring, nothing could break them. She admired that type.

Max didn't share her appreciation, however. He narrowed his eyes at them. "It's fine by me. There will be others in this town who will be willing to talk once I show them how serious I am."

Celeste hissed in a breath as Max's gun charged. He was serious about finding this girl—serious enough to kill to get what he wanted. Just like Terrance. Max was just like Terrance.

"No!" Celeste grabbed Max's hand. "Max, don't do it!"

Max glared at her. "Get off of me!"

"But Max, you don't have to do this—"

"I don't have time for nonsense." Max flung her to the ground. "Maybe Jordan and Jané were right about you. You are useless." He raised his gun to the dogs.

"But, Max! I know where she is," Celeste blurted.

Max halted. "What?" He turned to her.

"It's true!" Celeste used her chin to point at Melody. "She told me before."

Melody shook her head furiously. "No, I didn't."

"She lives on the edge of town in the forest. There's a road leading right to it. It couldn't be more than a ten minutes' walk away," Celeste blurted. Okay, so she made the last part up, but she couldn't see any teenager walking more than a mile to get anywhere. And judging by Melody's widened eyes and gaping mouth, Celeste had made a good guess.

And thankfully, Max seemed to think so too. After studying Melody's face, he raised his gun. "That was all you had to say. You should learn a little something about customer service."

"If you so much as touch one strand of fur on those two—"

"You're getting on my nerves." Max whacked Melody on the back of her head with the butt of his gun. She fell with a thud beside her bleeding father.

"Oh, no!" Celeste scrambled toward her, but Max stepped in her way.

"Get in the car, Celeste," he said.

"But, Max, why did you—" She froze when she saw his face. She couldn't argue with this command. If he was like Terrance, she was not too far off from turning his wrath toward her direction. She clamped her mouth shut, scrambled out of the grocery store, and climbed into the car.

She huddled in her seat, trembling. All this time she had been working for someone like Terrance. How couldn't she have seen it? She had to run. Hop out of the car, get a taxi, and escape. But then what would she do? Max still had her Freedom Certificate hostage. She was trapped. Celeste clutched her heart as realization dawned on her: she had traded one type of slavery for another.

Max walked out of the grocery store with a bit of a smile on his face. Jordan was nowhere to be seen. Celeste glanced around for him.

"Jordan's taking are of something for me," Max said, sensing her unasked question. He got in the car, started it, and turned to her. "Which road?"

"There." Celeste pointed to the road she'd seen before. "It's the only street going into the woods."

Max drove off. "Why didn't you tell me this sooner?"

"I wasn't sure before." Celeste ducked her head.

"And?"

"And nothing." Celeste refused to look him in the eye.

Max glanced at her out of the corner of his eye. "Why are you so nervous?"

"You have to ask after what you did in there?" Celeste swung toward him. "You nearly killed two people!"

"They wouldn't give me the information I needed."

Celeste grunted in disgust. "You're like Terrance Claybourne."

Max's ears stood straight up. "Don't ever compare me to him."

"Why not?" Celeste's fur rose. "He lies, cheats, steals, and kills to get what he wants too. What's the difference?"

"Let me ask you this." Max gripped the wheel harder. "If you had defied Terrance the way you defied me in there, would you still be alive now?"

Celeste opened her mouth to answer but shut it. "No." She hung her head. "If I didn't have this fur, he would have found some terrible way to torture me."

"Exactly."

"Even with my fur, he would have done something horrible." Celeste wrapped her arms around herself. "One of his favorite ways to punish me was to make me watch him strangle the life of someone else. Usually someone who stuck up for me."

"How is that a punishment for you?"

"Because if it wasn't for me, they wouldn't have gone through that!" Celeste ducked her head. "I'd have to watch him strangle someone innocent because of what I did. He'd have someone hold me back so I couldn't do anything. But then, he'd let me go, and I'd try to revive them."

"So you know CPR," Max muttered. "Useful."

"Nine times out of ten it was too late for them." Celeste bit her lips together. "And the times I was able to revive them, they'd hate me for what I made happen to them. It got so if I messed up, everyone would scramble to see who could tell Terrance first so they wouldn't have to share my punishment. I learned real quick not to count on anyone. No one would ever stick their neck out for me."

"Is that the reason you wouldn't tell me where the girl was? Trying to protect her since no one would protect you?"

"I didn't tell you because it's creepy," Celeste said.

"How so?"

"Because she's 12!"

"Fair point." Max exhaled through his nose. "My interest in her is purely scientific."

Celeste raised an eyebrow at him.

"Look . . . remember when we first met in Jelu? I wasn't only surveying damage there." Max's jaw clenched so hard his muscles twitched. "She was waiting for me to pick her up, but someone got ahold of her first. She was taken from *me*! I've been spending all this time trying to find her again."

"So . . . you're her legal guardian?" Celeste gulped. "Or . . . her master?"

"Not her master." Max's lips tightened to a thin line. "I don't own slaves. Never have, never will."

Celeste smiled. There was the Max she knew. "Then you are her guardian."

Max studied her a moment. "You can say that." But he didn't look at her when he said it. Celeste decided not to mention it. He was already gracious enough to answer all her questions. Better to sit tight and be quiet.

CHAPTER 35

"Here you go, Kat." Xena set a plate with a chicken sandwich and fries in front of Kathra. "Do you need to clutch your purse like that?"

"I'm leaving as soon as I finish lunch." Kathra kept her eyes glued on the new digi-book she had purchased. Her elbow rested on the table.

"If you don't like the food, tell me." Xena smacked her elbow off the table as she filled up her glass with lemonade. "I'll try and fix it."

"It's not the food. Your food's good." Kathra took a big bite of her sandwich. "Better than the restaurant's even."

"Then why do you look so gloomy?"

"I want to be with my friends." Kathra crossed her arms and pouted. "Everyone eats out when we have no school."

"If that's all, you should bring them over to eat." Xena sat with her sandwich at the table.

"You don't mind?"

"I like cooking. Maybe I can get the guys to dress up like waiters and serve you all." Xena took a bite of her sandwich. "It can be like a real fancy restaurant."

"I don't think your friends will go for it," Kathra said, slurping her lemonade.

"They will once I bend their arms behind their backs." Xena

flexed her bicep for emphasis. Though she had toned muscle, her arms were thin and lean. "Maybe we could do it for your birthday."

"You'd do that for me?" Kathra wiped her mouth. "But I thought you didn't like hanging out with me."

"You're my little sister, Kathra. Sure, you can be annoying at times, but you're cool."

"Really?" Kathra beamed, putting her book away in her purse. "Well, I'll invite Abby and Dephie. But not Feanne. We're not friends anymore."

"Again?" Xena took another bite of her sandwich. "Hmm . . . if I could invite anyone in the world to my birthday party, I'd invite the lady we met today . . . Celeste."

"Why?"

"She's so cool! She looks like she'd be the perfect big sister. Her car was amazing—"

"It wasn't her car," Kathra interjected, but Xena didn't listen.

"And she was so pretty with those big, green eyes."

"You said Vix was pretty."

"Vix is gorgeous, but Celeste is different." Xena felt her cheeks color a bit. "She's . . . like me. I've never seen another gray fox before. And the way she carried herself was so professional. She must be successful. Maybe she's a millionaire."

"Hm . . . I guess there's a lot of different types of people out there." Kathra munched on a fry. "People we'll never meet in Justin's Ridge."

"One day I'm going to go see them all." Xena leaned back in her chair. "I'll convince Mr. J.R. to take me with him and see the world."

Kathra rested her cheek on her hand again. "I'd rather stay here."

Someone banged on the front door, causing the sidelight glass to rattle.

"Who's that?" Kathra turned toward the banging.

"Who knows?" Xena walked to the front door. She raised her hand to open it when she caught the visitor's silhouette in the sidelight. A fox—male. She had never seen him in town before. Her ears angled back, and she locked the door as quietly as she could.

"Who's there?" Kathra crept up beside Xena, clutching her

purse.

Xena shrugged and put her finger to her lips. Maybe if they were quiet . . .

"I know you're in there, little girl!" came a male voice. It was smooth, yet anger had roughened it around the edges. "Open the door!"

Xena backed away from the door. "Go to the back."

"I want to talk to your parents about the damage you caused to my car!" the stranger said.

"Damage?" Xena halted. "Hey, I didn't do anything to your car!" she yelled through the door.

"Then why do I have a large dent in my driver's side door?"

Xena exchanged glances with Kathra who shrugged. "I didn't put a dent in your car."

The stranger sighed an exasperated sigh. "No need to keep lying, little girl. My assistant, Celeste, saw the whole thing and told me all about it."

Xena's fur rose, and the lights brightened in the house. She swung the door open. "I don't know what she said to you but . . ." She halted when she saw the red fox's nasty grin.

"Got ya," he said, his grin widening.

Xena turned to run.

"No, you don't." The fox caught her arm.

"Let me go!" Xena wriggled her arm in his grasp. "Kathra, run. Call the police!"

Kathra, eyes wide in terror, scrambled to the phone.

"Don't think so." The fox whipped a gun out of his jacket and shot Kathra in the back. She collapsed on the floor.

"Kathra!" Xena snarled at the stranger. She elbowed his stomach, followed it to a blow to his face with the back of her fist, and then roundhouse kicked him the stomach. He doubled over in pain, releasing her. She darted to Kathra. "Kathra! Kathra!"

"You little brat!" The stranger snarled.

Xena felt a sharp prick on her lower back. A tingling sensation spread throughout her body. A cold weight dampened her arms and legs, paralyzing her limbs. She collapsed. "Come on, legs. Move!" She tried to stand, tried to reach Kathra, but her legs wouldn't cooperate.

Her vision blurred—darkening to a point before it went black.

She passed out inches from reaching her sister.

* * *

"This is why I hate kids." Max set his laser pistol back in his jacket holster. He walked over to the gray kit and examined her fur. "It's more magnificent than I could have imagined." Then his eyes fell on the white-furred kit. "What a problem." He rubbed the back of his head. "I could leave her here, but she's a witness. Maybe I should . . ." He reached for his gun.

"Max, what's going on?" Celeste appeared at the door. She gasped. "Oh, my—" Her eyes widened. "Are they dead? Did you kill them? Why would you do that?"

Max didn't know why he jumped when he heard Celeste approach. "They're not dead. They're stunned. What kind of person do you take me for? Help me carry them." He swung the gray furred kit over his shoulder.

"But . . ." Celeste gazed at the white fox. She stooped down to pick her up but surreptitiously felt for a pulse. Max pretended not to notice. "I get what you want with her." She pointed at the gray-furred kit with her chin. "But what do you need with this one?" She struggled to hoist the girl.

Max shot her a glare. "Too many questions, Celeste."

"Sorry." Celeste said, following him out.

He led her out to the car and set the kit in the back seat. He arranged her to look like she fell asleep in the car, putting on her seatbelt to make it look legitimate. The stun should be strong enough to last them until they got to the high-speed transport chamber, where he'd give her enough sedatives to keep her unconscious until he could get her under proper lock and key at MFP. As for the white kit . . .

Max looked around. Celeste had paused in the front walk gazing into the distance.

"Max, look!" Celeste's eyes were fixed on a spot above the trees. "Smoke. I think there's a fire in town."

Max turned in the direction she was looking. Black smoke billowed above the trees. Looked like Jordan did his job well.

"I wonder what caught on fire." Celeste remembered herself and carried the white kit to the car.

"Who knows?" Max smirked. "There's always some crisis going on in small towns like this."

CHAPTER 36

J.R. closed his laptop computer and stretched out on the loveseat in Vix's apartment. The city lights twinkled through the windows as the stars would have if their light could have competed with the cityscape's.

Though they shared the same name, New Jelu was not at all like its predecessor. The old Jelu was a small town, much like Justin's Ridge. New Jelu was a city. J.R. felt its activity pulsating through him, making his muscles quiver in anticipation of a dangerous job.

He slouched in his seat and scratched his armpit.

"Men can be so disgusting." Vix walked out of her bedroom and put her hand on her hips. She was wearing a gray sweat suit, and her hair fell past the small of her back.

"I'm enjoying this time off. I haven't been able to do what I've wanted to in years. Those kids of mine . . ."

"Your kids?" Vix said. "You're not going to get distracted thinking about those brats, are you?"

"I'm a professional, Vix. I've got all the information I need for the job. Ol' Max is not going to know what hit him."

Vix eased down beside him. "We can get started tomorrow."

"Anything to eat?" J.R. said.

"What do I look like, a chef? Order something. Your turn to pay."

J.R. pulled his phone from his jacket. "What do you want?"

Vix draped herself over her couch and blew her hair out of her face. "Surprise me."

"Pizza it is, then." J.R. gazed at the phone, his fingers hovering over the buttons. When was the last time he'd had pizza from a restaurant? The Kid always cooked, and her pies were better than the takeout place's. Hmm . . . Xena . . . Kathra . . . He hadn't spoken to them for a few days . . . "I'll check on my kids first."

Vix jerked her head around. "Are you kidding me?"

J.R. pressed the power button on his phone. He had turned it off to prevent distractions while researching. As soon as the phone powered on, a jingle rattled its speakers. He glanced at the name flashing on the phone before he answered. It was Melody. "What's up, Mel?"

"Where have you been, J.R.?" Melody shouted so loud J.R. had to hold the phone away from his ear. "I've been trying to call you!"

"Been busy. I turned off my phone to—"

"I don't care! Xena's missing! So's Kathra! They're not at the house or with any of their friends! I've tried calling, and I can't reach them. The fox you told us about did something to them, and I can't leave the hospital because Dad's in rough shape and—"

J.R. sat up in his chair. "Whoa! Whoa! Whoa, Mel. You're going too fast."

"Xena and Kathra are gone, J.R." Melody spoke through her teeth. "Xena may have done something to the fox's car. He came in here furious! He tried to find her, and when we refused to tell him where she lived, he shot Dad and left someone who set our store on fire! They barely managed to get Dad and me out. He's in critical condition; you know how sick he's been lately."

J.R. fell silent. His lips receded from his teeth until they were all bared.

"J.R.?" Vix rested her hand on his shoulder. "Are you alright?"

J.R. shrugged her off. "I'm coming back now. Don't worry, Mel. I'll get them back. I swear I will."

"And when you do . . ." Melody's voice dropped to a growl. "Make him pay for this."

J.R. didn't respond. If he said something to her, he wouldn't be able to stop cursing for hours.

"What's going on?" Vix said.

"Sorry, Vix." J.R. spoke through his teeth. "I can't do the job with you."

"Why?"

"Someone kidnapped my kids. *Mine!*"

"Oh."

J.R. clenched his fists. "And you know what I do to anyone who muscles in on my territory."

Vix's eyes widened. "Badof's still in the hospital with a broken jaw."

"You can keep the research. Break in the GFG yourself and do it." J.R. swung a bag over his shoulder.

"I'll postpone the job till you can come with." Vix leaned back on her couch. "Only a fool would try to break into there without someone like you on the team."

J.R. halted. Breaking in as a team, huh? A smile came to his lips. "Hey, Vix."

"Hm?"

J.R. grinned so a sharp fang glistened in the light. "Mind if I use you as bait?"

CHAPTER 37

 $\mathbf{M}$ ax pulled into MFP on a clear night with a full moon. Instead of taking the road around to the parking garages, he drove up the main driveway to the main entrance. As he drove down the gravel driveway, he passed all sorts of exotic greenery. Dozens of flowers from all over the globe had been planted in shrub-enclosed gardens, and the gardeners had set up lights to change colors and illuminate the flowers in various shades of color depending on the time of year. Low green lawns, fenced in trees, and sculpted topiaries covered the grounds. And around the entire complex stood a high wall. A set of white marble stairs led from the driveway to the main entrance.

But Celeste didn't notice any of it. She was too taken up with Max's demeanor. When they had first picked up Xena, he had been so excited he could barely sit still. He had even turned on the radio and hummed tunes coming over the radio waves. She had been tickled to learn he loved the oldies. But once they reached the high-speed transport station, his smile faded. He turned the radio off, became snippy, and snarled more and more. At first Celeste thought it was another transport headache, but even after he had taken medicine his mood deteriorated. By the time they got to MFP, he was positively furious.

Celeste didn't know what she had done.

He pulled up to the front entrance and reached back to feel

Xena's neck. "Pulse is still strong." He flung himself back in his seat. "Then why won't she wake up? The stun should have worn off hours ago."

"Maybe she's allergic?" Celeste suggested.

Max threw open the door. "No one's allergic to a stun gun, Celeste." He rolled his eyes as he got out of the car, stomped to the back seat, and threw Xena over his shoulder.

"What about Kathra?" Celeste scrambled out of the car after him. "What am I supposed to do with her?"

"Who?" Max looked at her over his shoulder.

Celeste pointed at the white fox in the back seat. "Should I take her to the medical complex? She's not awake either."

"Do what you want with her." Max turned his back on her. "I don't care."

"Okay . . ." Celeste opened the car door as a van pulled up behind them.

"Oh, my goodness!" Tess squealed as she hopped out of the van. She rushed over to Max. "Look at it! It's magnificent!" She ran her hand the wrong way up Xena's fur.

"Isn't it, though?" Max grinned at her. "But we may have a problem. Set up the main lab for her."

"Yes, sir!" Tess balled up her fists and squealed again as she rushed inside.

"Who is this?" Jané climbed out of the van and approached Max and Xena.

"My daughter." Max walked up the stairs into the complex without another word.

Celeste halted, her breath catching. Why would he say something like that?

"Alright, Celeste." Jané put her hands on her hips. "Who is she really?"

Celeste thrust her nose in the air. "Didn't you hear him, Jané? It's his daughter." She climbed up the stairs.

Max was waiting for her inside. "I'm going to be busy for a while, so you may not see me around."

"Then what should I do all day?" Celeste asked, aware of Jané approaching behind her.

"What you've been doing." Max carried Xena down the hall, ignoring all the questioning looks he got as he walked past person after person.

"It's back to cleaning lady for you, huh?" Jané chuckled as she unpacked her things from the van. "So it goes with all those who aren't really in his confidence."

Celeste glared after her. She really hated Jané.

"Celeste." Max returned, carrying Xena. "It occurred to me . . . I don't have a way to contact you. Go get a cell phone in town, and text the number to me. I'll make sure everyone knows I'm leaving you in charge of office matters."

"You're putting her in charge?" Jané pushed passed Celeste.

"Of office matters, yes." Max turned to walk off. "Jordan will handle everything else."

Celeste smirked as Max walked away. "Who's in his confidence now?"

Jané shot her a glare before stomping away.

Once Jané was out of earshot, Celeste squealed. She had done it. She was in. Max did see her as a valuable asset to his team. And she had to remain so. First, she had a lot of work to do organizing Max's office after so many days gone. Plus she had to take care of the white . . .

The kit! Celeste raced back down the stairs. The kit was still in the back seat, unconscious. Celeste sighed as she looked at her. What in the world was she supposed to do with a child? Well, first thing was to get her checked out. At the very least, she'd be able to keep track of her location in the medical complex . . . at least for a little while.

CHAPTER 38

J.R. had left Vix in Jelu and returned to Justin's Ridge. After cleaning up the house so Melody and Mr. Withers could stay there while they rebuilt their store, he put together a task force to rebuild the buildings damaged by the fire, did some research on the likeliest place Max would have taken Xena and Kathra, and met up with Vix again in Jelu.

"It's a two week drive to MFP," J.R. said to her as he packed up his speeder with his tools. "We'll travel as fast as we can. Once we get there, I'll have to spend a day or two doing recon to find the best way to get in . . ."

Vix pouted as she leaned against her speeder. "Tell me again why I'm helping you rescue your brats?"

"Because MFP is where the top researchers at the GFG Corporation keep all their top secret goodies. Anything in there is worth at least twice as much as what your client wants you to steal. And knowing Terrance Claybourne, he just wants to get back at Max." J.R. growled. "We have that in common."

"More money? I like the sound of that." Vix gave a toothy grin. "But if you're in such a hurry, why not take the transport tunnels? I don't think I've ever seen you take one."

"Because they're monitored." J.R. held his hands like a camera. "They take your picture before you go in."

"Ah." Vix nodded. "That might be why I always have heat on

me when I come out of those things."

"You are a notorious criminal, Vix."

"Not half so notorious as you." Vix flicked his whiskers. "Don't worry, Big Guy. We'll get your brats back."

"Thanks, Vix. You're a peach. A greedy one, but a peach all the same."

Vix wrinkled her nose in a smile.

CHAPTER 39

Taking care of Max's office wasn't as glamourous as Celeste thought it would be. It was basically organizing papers into those Max had to sign and those he didn't, answering phones, and handling problems with the most obvious of solutions. Still, it was fun. People respected her; they listened to her. Nobody treated her like a slave-girl. Since Max said so, everyone thought she was somebody. Best of all, her promotion had come with a pay raise. Her papers would be hers in no time.

She hummed a tune as she walked into Max's office ready for another day of fruitful work.

"Oh!" Celeste halted.

Max sat at his desk with his fingers laced, eyes narrowed to a slit. His whiskers twitched in time with the clock's second hand tick.

"Good . . . morning, Max." Celeste paused to examine him. "Are you okay?"

"No." Max's whiskers stiffened. "I'm pissed. Close the door."

Celeste eased the door shut, mentally rummaging through her memories of the last few days. She hadn't done anything wrong to make him mad, had she? No. Not that she could remember.

"I am not in my research lab right now, Celeste." Max stood, making his chair spin, and skirted his desk. "Why am I not in my research lab?"

"I-I don't know."

"Because of you." Max thrust his nose in her face. "Because I was stupid enough to trust you."

"W-what did I do?"

"The box. The one I asked you to get in Justin's Ridge." Max slammed his palm on his desk. "Something is missing from it, and you're the last one who had possession of it."

"I didn't do it!" Celeste fought to keep her tail from slipping between her legs. She failed. "I didn't touch the box. It was closed when I picked it up. I swear!"

"Then what happened to it, Celeste?"

"I-I don't know!" Celeste felt her position—the respect, the authority, and her papers—slipping away. Her eyes drifted to the vault where Max has stashed her certificate. She worked so hard to get here, but if Max sent her away . . .

No! She jerked her eyes back to Max's face. Don't look at the vault. Never let the one who has power over you know what you want. He'd use it against you.

But it was too late. Max glanced over his shoulder at the vault. "Oh, right!" A nasty grin slid onto his face. "Your papers are in there. Well, if you want them, you better get me what's mine. Now!"

Celeste flinched. But her mind whirled. If only she knew what he was after . . . "W-what's are you missing?"

Max examined her, his eyes hard. Finally, he exhaled through his nose. "A disk. A digi-book."

"A book?" Celeste let her ears angle forward. "You mean you ordered 144,000 computer chips for one book?"

"Focus, Celeste!" Max slammed his palm on his desk again. "I need the book!"

"I don't know. I didn't see a—wait!" Celeste waved her index finger in the air. "I noticed the box had been opened before I got there. The owner guy said there was a holo-disk mixed up in all those computer chips, so he replaced it with another of the same type."

Max kicked his desk. "The frickin' idiot! Leave it to a flippin' small town hick to ruin everything!"

Celeste bit her lips together. If Max had gone through so much trouble to get the disk, it must be important. The owner had said he'd give them their money back within 30 days, but that wouldn't help find the disk. He'd already sold it. To—

"Oh, Max, I know where it is!" Celeste clapped her hands together.

Max swung around to face her. "What?"

"At least, I know who bought it. Kathra. The white kit we brought with Xena . . ." She trailed off. What *did* Max do with Xena?

"Glad we brought her, then." Max sighed as he collapsed against his desk. "Where is she?"

"In the medical complex. She woke up last night."

"Find out where she put the disk and let me know." Max pushed himself off the desk. "I'll send someone to get it."

"But what should I do with Kathra now that she's awake?"

"I'll let you deal with it."

"Okay." Celeste watched Max walk out of the office. "Please, oh, please, Kathra. Don't hide this disk from me. We need it for both our sakes." She took a deep breath before trotting out of the office herself.

CHAPTER 40

When Kathra had woken up in the middle of the night, she had no idea where she was. So she screamed. She screamed and yelled and cried until the nurses came in to calm her down. They had said she was in a hospital—she had been unconscious for several days. The last thing Kathra remembered was the fox breaking into her house. She didn't know what happened after or where Xena was.

Xena! Where was she? Though she asked everyone who came in, nobody knew where her sister was. She had even tried the communicator. Nothing. A weight fell on Kathra's chest. Her sister was gone. She'd never see her or Justin's Ridge or Mr. J.R. again. At the realization, tears came to her eyes. She sobbed and sobbed and refused to be consoled.

Which was what she was doing now. She sat on her hospital bed with her knees drawn to her chest. She was alone. No one knew where she was. Not even she knew where she was. If only she had her scanner . . .

There was a tap on her door. She looked up. Who would be knocking on her door, seeing as it was locked from the outside? Anyone who wanted to come in, came in. No need to ask for her permission.

But the person seemed to be waiting for a response, so Kathra said, "Come." Her voice was scratchy from all the crying.

"Hi, Kathra." A gray vixen peeked in. "Do you remember me?" She slipped in.

All Kathra's tears dried in the heat of the rage washing over her. "You're the vixen from the computer store we went to! You lied about Xena to your boss! You—" She gasped as a new thought came to her. "You *kidnapped* me!"

"No, no! That's not true." Celeste waved her hands. On one of them was Kathra's favorite pink purse.

Kathra pointed at it. "And you stole my purse!"

"I was bringing it back to you." Celeste offered it to her. "They told me to hold onto it until you woke up."

Kathra snatched the purse. She yanked it open to check its contents. Everything was there—her compact with the plastic blush, her scanner, her new digi-book, and her pack of lip gloss. She snapped the purse shut.

"Everything's in there." Celeste placed a hand on her chest. "I kept it safe for you. No one went through your things."

"Am I supposed to say, 'thank you'?"

Celeste tilted her head to the side, allowing her hair to cascade over her shoulder. She gave a sad smile as if Kathra was a small child who had no idea how the world worked. "I understand why you're mad at me, but can I tell you something about myself? Something personal?"

Kathra blinked. Celeste wanted to share something personal with her? A secret? Kathra loved secrets; keeping one made her seem more grown up. Before she realized what she was doing, Kathra had leaned closer to Celeste. She had something inviting . . . soothing about her . . .

With a smile that set Kathra at ease, Celeste sat on the bed beside her. "I was a slave," she said.

"Really?" Kathra's eyes widened.

"I belonged to a terrible man named Terrance Claybourne." Celeste gripped her hands tightly. "He was evil . . . cruel . . . devious. I had to escape even if it meant he'd kill me if he caught me. I risked everything to run away."

"But . . . how did you get a job if you're a slave?"

"I met Max." Celeste smiled as if she was in a spring meadow on a warm day. "He paid my debt and bought my freedom."

"So that's why you work for him?"

"Partly. He didn't do it as a gift. It was a loan, sort of. I have to pay him back." Celeste sighed, and it seemed as if the world turned gray. "I have over $400,000 to repay."

"That's a lot of money."

Celeste nodded. "And if I don't he'll send me back to Terrance Claybourne who will kill me for what I did. So you see, I had to do what I did back there. I'm sorry if I hurt you or your sister."

"My sister! Xena!" At the mention of Xena, the air Celeste had woven around her story broke. "Can you take me to her?"

Celeste shook her head. "I don't know where she is, but . . . I can try and find out."

"Please." Kathra clutched Celeste's hands, not afraid or enraged anymore. "Please find her."

"I will. I promise." Celeste patted Kathra's hands. "But there's something I need from you first. Remember when I saw you in the computer store? You bought a book."

"Uh, huh! It's a book of fairy tales. It tells the story and then details how scientists are trying to figure out the truth behind them. I'm in the middle of the story about Silver Foxes."

"Silver Foxes?" Celeste paused for a moment, her smile frozen. "The book is mine. It was supposed to be included in the box I picked up, but it got mixed up somehow. Please tell me where it is."

Kathra clutched her purse to her chest. "But I'm not done with it, yet. And I paid for it."

"It belongs to Max, and he's mad he doesn't have it. If I don't get it back, he'll send me away, and—" Celeste paused a moment, staring at her hands on her lap. In a moment, she looked up at Kathra, her eyes hard as emeralds. "And if he finds out you kept it from him, who knows what he'll do to your sister. You don't want to be the cause of her pain, do you?"

Kathra gasped. She shook her head.

"Then tell me where it is."

Kathra took a shaky hand and pulled out the disk.

"You have it with you?" Celeste gazed at it.

Tears pooled in Kathra's eyes. The thought of Xena getting hurt because she wanted to read her book . . .

"Oh, Kathra, I'm sorry." The hardness in Celeste's face melted away. "Look . . ." She looked around, tip-toed to the door, and peeked outside. "Listen," she said her voice lowered to a whisper. "I'll come back in five minutes. Why don't you finish your story? When I come back, I'll get the disk."

"But my sister. Will Max—"

"I won't tell." Celeste put a finger on her lips. "What Max doesn't know won't hurt him, right?" She winked at Kathra. "Five minutes." Then she slipped out.

Kathra didn't have the heart to read the story after Celeste left—not if it meant Xena could get hurt. Instead she waited for Celeste to return and handed it to her. Celeste took the disk, said some comforting things to her, and slipped out, leaving Kathra alone.

It was only after the door closed that the question dawned on Kathra: what if Celeste had played her somehow—manipulated the entire meeting to get Kathra help her find the disk she wanted? With a shudder, Kathra threw off the idea. She didn't want to believe she could be so easily swayed. Or that someone could play on her emotions so readily. Besides, the thought of someone as innocent looking as Celeste molding Kathra into whatever she wanted sent chills up Kathra's spine.

CHAPTER 41

Max ran his hands over his hair as he made his way back to the laboratories. Hopefully, Celeste would be able to find the location of the disk. But if it was hidden in Justin's Ridge, it could be days before he could get his hands on it.

He growled through his nose. Nothing was going right since he got back from that stupid town. For seven years he had been searching for the fox kit, all the while planning how he would unlock the secrets hidden in her fur. The blood and enzyme tests, as well as the DNA mapping were all underway, and he had set up a series of physicals, X-rays, and CAT Scans for her. Every chemical Max could think of would be injected into her in order to document how she reacted to each one. Every part of her, inside and out, was to be measured, categorized, and catalogued.

But there was a hitch. She had not yet woken up from the stun he had given her ten days ago, which meant all the plans he had for her were at a standstill.

"I've got to figure this out." Max muttered as he marched down the hall.

"Talking to yourself again?" Jordan fell into step beside Max.

"What do you need, Jordan?"

Jordan handed him a tablet. "Sign."

Max did so. "You could have left it with Celeste, you know. She would have put it with all the other things I need to sign. She even has the authority to sign minor documents herself."

Jordan grunted through his nose.

"Problem?"

"It's Celeste—"

"Oh." Max let it roll off his back. "I know you don't like her, Jordan. But you don't have to like her to work with her."

"That's not my problem."

"Then what is?"

"You are." Jordan pulled Max to a stop. "You're giving her too much power. First, she cleaned your office, and that was fine. But now she has authority to make decisions in your place? Signing your documents?"

Max continued down the hall, forcing Jordan to keep up with him. "You, Jané, and Tess all have the same authority in different capacities—"

"There's a big difference between us and her."

"What's that?"

"She's a glorified slave-girl! She doesn't know anything, and she's too hard to read. I can never tell what she's thinking. You should not be putting so much in her hands."

Max halted. "Are you telling me how to do my job?"

Jordan stiffened. "No. But the way you're coddling her makes me think you're grooming her for Phase Two."

"I was considering it."

"We're using Jané."

"We were," Max said. "And now we might not."

"What is wrong with you?" Jordan stared at Max as if he had green antennae shooting out of his hair. "Ever since *she* came, you've been going off your nut. This is something you should have discussed with me. I am your second-in-command. I care as much about the success of Phase Two as you do."

"I don't have to discuss anything with you, Jordan." Max narrowed his eyes. "And no one could care more about the success of Phase Two than me."

"But why would you make such a critical change when we are so close? Jané knows exactly what to do. She's ready."

"Jané is not . . . she's not . . ." Max gestured with his hands. "I'm not sure what it is she's not, but whatever she lacks Celeste has it. People trust Celeste for no apparent reason which is what I need."

"You're going to regret this decision to trust her, Max."

"We'll see."

"Max, Max! I got it!" Celeste sprinted down the hall accompanied by the "pok-pok" of her heels. "I have the disk!"

"That was quick," Max said.

"Turns out she had it in her purse." Celeste looked at the disk in her hands. "*Truth behind the Legends*. Is that it?"

"That's the one." Max took it from her. "You have no idea what I've been through to get my hands on this."

"A book of fairy tales?" Jordan crossed his arms.

"I would have had it sooner, but I let her finish reading the story she was on." Celeste held her hands behind her back. "It was the one about Silver Foxes."

Max noted her eyes never left his face. She was fishing for something . . .

But before Max could address it, Jordan burst out, "Silver Foxes? That tears it! Max, you have to stop!"

"Stop what?" Max turned his attention to Jordan. He could deal with Celeste at his leisure.

"This obsession you have with gray-furred foxes!"

"Obsession?" Celeste's ears stood on end.

Max chuckled. "I do not have an obsession."

"Oh, yeah?" Jordan's tail flicked his legs. "What about the name you chose for this organization? GFG—Gray Fox Group?"

"I chose it because gray foxes are rare and unique—an anomaly among their normal counterparts—as is this company."

Jordan raised an eyebrow. "Then what about Celeste?"

"What about Celeste?" Max said, acutely aware Celeste was watching this exchange. "She came to me. And I don't care one lick about her fur. I hold her to the same standard as anyone else. Don't I, Celeste?"

Celeste nodded.

"Then what about the rumors?" Jordan raised his nose into the air. "They say you think you have a Silver Fox in your laboratories. That it's the reason you're always down there lately."

"Really?" Max pressed his lips together. Someone in the laboratories had a big mouth.

"People are going to think you're crazy," Jordan said, and when

Max didn't respond added, "They'll stop following you—"

"People will keep following me as long as I give them what they think they need." Max glared at Jordan. "And I'd appreciate you squelching rumors instead of taking them seriously. Now, don't you have a job to do?"

"Yeah. I do." Jordan turned away from them. He shot a glare at Celeste as he marched down the hall.

Celeste hung around after he had left, absently stroking her fur.

Max rolled his eyes. He didn't feel like dealing with her at the moment. "Something you want, Celeste?"

"Well . . . um . . . no . . ."

"Then I suggest you get back to work." Max continued his trek toward the laboratories.

"Do you?" Celeste called after him.

Max stopped. "Do I what?"

Celeste trotted over to him. She looked up the hall then down it before whispering, "Do you think you have a Silver Fox in there?"

A heavy sigh tore out of him. He didn't want to have this conversation with her. Not yet. But if he didn't squash her curiosity now, it could grow out of control before he was ready to use her. And if he had to get rid of her—all his work grooming her would go down the drain. And she was working out so well . . .

"Because it would make sense if you did," Celeste said before he could make up his mind.

"How do you figure?"

"It would explain why you went through such lengths to get Xena." Celeste ran her hands over her fur. "You didn't give two kicks about my fur, but as soon as you saw hers you went crazy for it. And it would make sense why she's down there. That is where you're keeping her, right?"

Max nodded.

Celeste glanced in the direction of the laboratories, her ears falling.

"I take it you don't approve?"

"I know what it's like to only be valued because of your fur." Celeste gripped her arm close to her body. "It's not pleasant. I feel for her."

Max bit his bottom lip. This seemed like a critical turning point. Should he take a chance on her . . . ?

"Celeste." Max took a step closer to her. "If Silver Foxes existed and if I found one, don't you think it would be my duty to extract all of her fur's secrets?"

"Secrets?" Celeste turned her big, green eyes to Max.

"According to the stories, Silver Foxes had the ability to manipulate electricity, magnetics, and in some stories they could fly. If they do exist, why should those powers be reserved for the select few? Why should they get to keep it to themselves? Why can't we all benefit." Max turned to Celeste with his brightest smile on his face. "I've been trying to develop bioelectrical technology for years—yes, based on the Silver Foxes legends. Imagine a world where you didn't have to physically interact with a machine. All you had to do was think about a task, and it would be done. It would revolutionize the security industry! It could have military applications—devices keeping you and your freedom safe."

Max took a moment to study to Celeste to see if she was following his vision. Judging by the way her eyes sparkled and the wide smile on her face, he was painting the right picture.

"I'm not holding the girl to have her on display." Max raised his hands to the ceiling. "It is my duty to do whatever it takes to benefit our world. And that vixen is the key to it."

"Oh, wow!" Celeste raised her eyes to the ceiling. Max could almost see the idealistic, utopian world she was generating in her mind. Time to bring it crashing down.

"Of course if you're against that sort of thing," Max turned his back on her. "I'll have to let you go."

"No!" Celeste blurted at the top of her lungs. She clutched his arms. "I don't want to go! Don't send me away!"

Max smiled. That had been easier than he thought it would be. "So you're on board?"

Celeste nodded.

"But you don't believe the girl is a Silver Fox?"

Celeste studied the floor a moment. "I believe you think she is."

"Alright, then." Max headed down the hall. "Meet me tomorrow morning at 8:30. You can decide for yourself. Until then, back to work."

"Yes, Max."

"Oh, and Celeste?"

Celeste turned to look at him.

"This is classified. No one is to know what I told you." Max gave her a smile. "Not even Jordan."

A smile spread over Celeste's face. She nodded before turning to skip down the hall.

Max grinned at her retreating form. He didn't know what Jordan had been talking about. Celeste was all too easy to read.

CHAPTER 42

It was 8:25 A.M. when Celeste walked into Max's office. Max sat at his desk, reading the disk Celeste had retrieved for him.

"You aren't late, Celeste, but you're cutting it a little close." Max rose to his feet and walked passed her.

"Sorry." Celeste scurried after him. "I had a few things to take care of before my schedule could be cleared for the morning."

"I'm going to reiterate, Celeste, what you are going to see today is classified." Max paused to look into her eyes. "You've seen how I handle people who defy me. I don't want to have to do it to you."

Celeste swallowed hard. She nodded and scampered after him as he strode down the hallway again. He led her to a corridor with an arched sign that read, "MFP Research Laboratories, Authorized Personnel Only," over it. The door had been shut.

Max placed his hand on the scan pad to the right. The door slid open, and they walked into a white hallway. A purple light washed over them.

"How pretty!" Celeste held her hands out in the light. It tinted her fur violet.

A smile tugged at Max's lips as he watched her. "It's ultraviolet light. It eradicates viruses, bacteria . . . anything that could contaminate my labs."

The light faded, and he continued to lead her passed closed

doors to another locked door. Max stood still in front of it. A warm wave of red light caressed their forms.

Celeste let her mouth curl into a pout. "This one's not as nice."

Max chuckled. "It's an access scan."

"Unauthorized personnel detected," said a digital voice.

Celeste started. She glanced around, but Max stood as still as stone. "Add unauthorized personnel to access list," he said.

"Authorized User Access ID required."

"User Access ID: A855679," Max said.

"Access ID confirmed," the computer said. "Unauthorized Personnel, please place your hand on the handprint scanner and state your name."

"Oh, um . . ." Celeste placed her hand on the same place Max had. "Celeste . . . Sinceré."

"Please confirm personnel information: Celeste Sinceré; employee number: 54323-6; age: 22; birthday: June 21; date of freedom: April 22 . . ." The computer continued to rant off her information.

Celeste's mouth dropped open. "How does it know?"

Max didn't answer. When the computer finished listing her information, he said, "Confirmed."

"Access level?" the computer asked.

"Level 5," Max said.

"Access list modified," the computer said. "New User Access ID added: R397287." The door slid open.

"Keep a note of your Access ID, Celeste." Max strode through the lab entrance. "It's the only way you can access anything in here."

"Oh, I . . ." Celeste scurried after him. "I wasn't paying attention."

"Always pay attention." Max didn't even look at her. "I'll give it to you again later. You now have limited access to this lab, but do not come down here without my knowledge and do not tell anyone I gave you access." He narrowed his eyes. "Understand?"

"Yes, Max."

"Good."

Celeste walked through the door. A cold blast made her fur fluff out, and soon she was shivering. "Why is it so cold in here?"

"For the equipment." Max handed her a white lab coat, and

donned one himself.

Celeste gazed at it before putting it on. It looked like Isha's lab coat. Celeste let her ears fall. She hadn't thought about Isha in years. She hoped she wasn't Terrance's new favorite.

"Keep up, Celeste." Max had donned black rubber gloves. Looking around, Celeste saw more hanging on the walls along with the lab coats and black rubber boots lined up on the floor. She scampered to join Max.

Beakers, Bunsen burners, centrifuges, computers, and other bright, steel contraptions Celeste had no knowledge of filled the tables set up around the lab. Max had stopped in front of a chamber that ran the height of the room. It was made of metal and had a glass front. All around the edges of the chamber ran multi-colored wires. Scientists in white lab coats and black rubber gloves scrambled up and down scribbling on clipboards or tapping on computers.

"Max!" One of the scientists rushed up to him. "Take a look at this." He pointed to the chamber.

Max leaned in to see what he was pointing at. Celeste peered in over his shoulder. Xena was hanging inside, suspended by fasteners around her hands and feet. Her breathing was deep and even, and her head bowed, making her chin rest on her chest.

But that wasn't what made Celeste cry out. It was her fur. It had become silver. Not merely shiny gray or shimmery, but a dull sort of silver—like scratched, polished jewelry.

"Max, how'd you make her fur like that?" Celeste swung around to him. "What did you do to her?"

"Not a thing." Max read a clipboard handed to him by a scientist. "Haven't been able to. You're looking at her natural fur."

"H-how is this possible?" Celeste gazed up at Xena's sleeping face.

"The only difference between her and us is the amount of metals she has." Max handed the clipboard back. "She was born with a genetic disorder that causes her to store excess amounts of it in her fur. Enough to conduct electricity."

"As a matter of fact, the machine is pumping 1500 volts into her with no harmful effects." A lynx stepped forward. "She is able to conduct the electricity through her fur, and will one day be able to manipulate it."

"Manipulate electricity?" Celeste gasped. "She really is a Silver Fox."

"Our research seems to indicate the particular properties we are interested in don't reveal themselves until after puberty," the lynx said. "But she's 12 and changing fast. I'm curious to see how far we can push her."

"Be careful you don't let your scientific curiosity get the better of you, Dr. Marine. I want you to experiment on her, not kill her," Max said, crossing his arms. "You had no idea she could survive such voltage."

The lynx pushed up her glasses. "This is a carefully monitored situation, sir. We watched her vitals. We would not let her die."

"See that you don't." Max glowered at her. "She's the only one in existence, and I have my own agenda to pursue."

Celeste tuned out of Max and Dr. Marine's conversation and focused on Xena. A Silver Fox. The legends claimed a Silver Fox was born gray and didn't achieve its powers until they proved themselves. Maybe there was some truth in it. A few weeks ago, her fur was gray, but now . . .

Celeste rested her hand on the glass. Poor thing. All this fuss over her fur . . . Celeste knew what it was like. When Xena woke up, she'd be in for a rude awakening—

Xena's head bobbed. Celeste jerked her hand away from the glass. Xena's head swayed slightly. Her eyes twitched before fluttering open. For a moment, they drifted around, not settling on anything. She shut her eyes and opened them again. This time they focused. She must have understood her situation now for she jerked against the fasteners and cried out. But Celeste heard nothing. The chamber was soundproof.

Then Xena's eyes rested on Celeste. She said Celeste's name . . . Celeste saw her mouth move—pronouncing the syllables making up her name. A mute cry for help.

Celeste bit her bottom lip. The button to release her was right there on the control panel of the machine. All she had to do was push it, and Xena could use her Silver Fox powers to escape.

But where would it leave Celeste? Max would be furious if she helped the only Silver Fox in existence to escape. He'd get rid of her for sure. And just when he had let her into his confidence— showed her things he hadn't even shown Jordan and Jané. She had found a place in the GFG Corporation. She couldn't lose everything now.

Celeste turned her back on the Silver Fox. "Max?" He was deep in conversation and didn't answer her. "Max!"

"What, Celeste?"

Celeste pointed at the chamber. "She's awake."

The Silver Fox gazed at Celeste with her mouth agape. Celeste narrowed her eyes. What did she expect? You can't count on anyone to stand up for you. It was a lesson Xena had better learn fast.

Max approached the chamber even as the Silver Fox cowered against her bonds. "Hello, there, sweetheart." He placed his hand on the glass.

The Silver Fox shrank down, her short breaths making her tremble.

"I'm sorry, ladies and gentlemen." Max shut the machine off. "I've got to let her rest so I can run my own tests on her."

"But sir," Dr. Marine said, "you will bring her back?"

"Of course. I have to unlock all her secrets." Max turned to Celeste. "Go back to the office now, Celeste. I'll be there soon."

"Right." Celeste turned to leave.

"And Celeste?"

She turned.

Max put a finger to his lips. "Remember, this is our little secret." He winked at her.

"I won't tell a soul." Celeste said, her smile so wide it hurt her cheeks. She nearly skipped her way out of the laboratory.

CHAPTER 43

"There's MFP." J.R. lay on his stomach on the edge of a hill looking through binoculars at Max's complex in the distance. The complex covered several acres and was surrounded by a brick wall. It was bordered on one side by one of the many towns Max controlled and on the other by dense woods. Everything Max could ever need from laboratories to training grounds to temporary housing for the workers he had freed from slavery was in this complex.

"MFP . . . MFP . . ." Vix lay beside him looking through her own binoculars. She was wearing her "work clothes"—a dark green shirt a size too small and black cargo pants that caressed her shape in all the right places. She was a good companion to have on a job like this, but J.R. could not figure why she was repeating the name of the complex over and over.

"The place looks so familiar to me. And the name MFP . . . MFP . . ." Vix muttered, her tail waving back and forth in thought. "MFP . . . Wait! This is the Municipal Freedom Project building! It's where they house all the slaves the GFG Corporation frees, right?"

J.R. raised an eyebrow at her. "You just put it together now?"

"You brought me all the way out here for nothing, you bastard!" Vix punched his shoulder. "You only wanted me as a distraction so you could get your brats. You lied to me!"

"The housing stuff's a front, Vix." J.R. continued peering through his binoculars. "It's also where Max keeps all the stuff too controversial or too illegal for his company to have a public hand in."

"Oh." Vix settled down back next to J.R. "Pretty smart of him."

"You have no idea." J.R. set his binoculars down. "Max really has a racket going. It seems like a bad idea . . . spending all that money on freeing slaves and reeducating them and stuff, but he's created a super loyal work force."

"Full of janitors and construction workers." Vix stood to dust off the front of her pants. "Good for him."

"You have no idea how much power janitors and construction workers have—one knows exactly how a place was built, the other has the keys to it," J.R. said. "But he doesn't stop there. Some of his 'Freedom Workers' have moved up to government positions, high-level business positions, military positions . . . he's got people all over the place loyal to him. It's a brilliant plan."

"Guess we shouldn't underestimate him." Vix turned to the complex. "How long until we get there?"

"Four hours. We'll have to travel around. If we set foot in town Max will know about it five minutes later."

"As long as you get me in I'll do my part, but I still don't get why Max would want those brats." Vix adjusted the gadgets hanging from her belt. "You're dangerous when someone touches your stuff."

"I don't know . . ." J.R.'s voice dropped to a growl. "But when I do come across Max . . ." He cracked his knuckles.

"Hope someone is around to plan his funeral."

J.R. glared in the direction of Max's complex. "Let's go."

"Lead the way," Vix said.

* * *

J.R. barely gave the towers surrounding Max's complex a glance, but Vix gazed up at one them with wide eyes. They had left their speeders in the woods bordering the building and now stood at the base of the wall surrounding it. A series of gates were interspersed along the circumference. The main gate were for visitors and

181

unauthorized personnel, like delivery persons. They were checked, scanned, and issued ID cards which were linked to the alarm system. Should a visitor wander into the wrong place, the alarm would sound and Max's guards would swarm to the area of intrusion.

J.R. smirked. He had been the cause of that upgrade.

He skirted the main gate and approached a secondary gate at the west side—one for employees only.

"What are you doing, J.R.?" Vix followed him. "You can't get into this place through the gates. They're all electronic and tamper-proof. I know; I've tried."

"Only if you don't have the right tools." J.R. pulled a card from his belt of tools and swiped it in a card reader. With a long beep the gate swung open. "Stay close and shut up."

"Snippy."

J.R. and Vix approached the building and snuck around to a side door, where J.R. again used his device to open the door.

"Nifty card," Vix said. "Where'd you get it?"

"Sherd." J.R. squinted into the light as he entered the building. "Pretend like you belong here. We're supposed to have been checked by security five times before reaching here, so everyone will assume we belong. Once we get some appropriate uniforms for this department, we'll be able to go anywhere without trouble. I know where they keep the extras."

"See, there's a reason I chose you to do this with me," Vix said as she trotted to keep up with him.

J.R. ducked into a closet where he and Vix donned lab coats. Once done, he peeked out to make sure the hall was clear. "This is it, Vix. Here's what I want you to do. Down there is the R and D testing lab. If you want to find something to satisfy your client, go there. I'm going to find Xena and Kathra. It won't be easy to transport my kids without getting caught so when I give you the signal, make a big stink to attract as much attention as you can. Then get outta there. I won't stop to get you if you get caught."

"You're a real gentlemen, J.R." Vix sniffed. "But I suppose it's the least I can do since you got me in. Though, I'm going to get the true story of where those brats came from one of these days."

J.R. grunted. "I doubt it."

"We'll see, Big Guy." Vix waved back at J.R. as she walked

down the hall he indicated.

J.R. watched her go before creeping back out into the hallway. According to Sherd, Max had indeed brought two girls to the complex. He couldn't pinpoint the location of one of them, but the other had been in the medical ward. He clenched his teeth as he headed off. If they had done anything to hurt either Xena or Kathra, this entire complex would be reduced to rubble by morning. J.R. swore it to himself.

CHAPTER 44

Kathra pulled her knees to her chest and wrapped her arms around them. To the casual observer, she looked like a timid, shivering kit, overwhelmed by the way her life had been altered in the last month. Kidnapped, stripped from everything she knew, only to wake up to a massive headache and severe nausea ought to reduce any eight year old to a blubbering mass of nerves.

But in reality, Kathra was scheming.

With no one but herself to count on, she had to escape—find a way out of the hospital, get to a phone, and call Mr. J.R. to come get her. She didn't even know where she was, but she had her scanner. The minute Celeste had left her, Kathra ran a thorough scan of the place. But to no avail. There was something blocking the scan from accessing the GPS satellite, so she couldn't tell where in the world she was. She was, however, able to generate a map of the complex itself. With no context, though, all those halls and rooms meant nothing.

But the scan did ping something else. Xena. She still had the communicator J.R. was working on in her ears. The signal was weak, coming from somewhere on the other side of the complex, but she was here. When she had seen that blip, Kathra had clutched her scanner and cried from sheer happiness. She had to get to Xena. But how? And how to get out of here?

Sure, she had been locked in this room, but shortly after being able to walk around, Kathra found the window hadn't been locked. The day she had discovered it, she nearly jumped out into the garden. But a flashlight stopped her. Guards, of course. If she was going to escape and get to her sister, she had to figure out when and where the guards would be at any given moment. Again, she had turned to her scanner for the answer. After a few days of watching the guards' movements, she had their schedule down to the minute. And today was going to be the day she escaped. Kathra watched her scanner as the usual blips made their way around the building. Just a little more . . .

A new blip appeared on the screen, coming straight for her door. Shoot! Could it be Celeste already? Celeste had been the only one to visit Kathra in all the days she had been here. Xena had been right about her. Celeste had been kind and sweet, bringing Kathra treats and chatting to her every day. But as nice as she was, Kathra had to escape. Hopefully, Celeste wouldn't stay long.

Kathra shoved her scanner beneath the sheets and stared at the door. A silhouette, much larger than Celeste's, appeared in the door's window. It eased it open, slipped inside, and closed it.

Kathra gasped. Though clad in a lab coat, she'd recognize those pointed ears anywhere.

"Mr. J.R.!" Kathra launched herself at him, barely giving him enough time to turn and catch her.

"Kat!" J.R. held her close to him.

As soon as he did—as soon as Kathra smelled his fur and felt his warmth—a sob escaped her. She didn't mean to cry . . . she knew J.R. hated tears . . . but after so long being alone in this strange place, to feel safe and comfortable . . .

"It's okay, Kitten. I'm here." J.R. patted her back. He didn't even tell her to knock off the wailing. "I'm sorry I left you, but I'm here now."

Kathra got a hold of herself. She pulled away from him and dried her tears. Now was not the time to cry. She had to act. "Xena's here, too, Mr. J.R.! We have to go get her."

"Any clue where she is?" J.R. set her on the bed.

"Only this." Kathra showed him her scanner. "See? Her communicator is over there. But the signal's weak. I can't tell exactly which room she's in or how to get there. And she won't answer me."

J.R. studied the map displayed on the scanner. "But it corresponds to the Restricted Laboratories. That can't be right."

"My scans are never wrong, Mr. J.R."

J.R. played with the fur on his chin. "Hmmm . . . If we can get closer to the signal, can you get a more accurate scan?"

"For sure!"

"Then the only problem is how to get access to the labs . . ."

A new silhouette appeared at the door. The door opened a crack, and Celeste's voice drifted in. "No, I understand, Doctor . . . I'll move her soon."

J.R. put a finger to his lips and hid in the bathroom.

Kathra scrambled back into bed as Celeste stepped in. "Huh? The door wasn't locked. Kathra?"

"Hi, Miss Celeste." Kathra waved at her.

"There you are!" Celeste walked over to her. "How are you feeling today?"

"Good."

"Excellent." Celeste held her hands behind her back. "Guess what? The doctor says you can be discharged. How'd you like to be my roomie for a while?"

"I'd rather see my sister," Kathra said, trying not to look at the bathroom. "Can't you take me to her?"

Celeste inhaled through her teeth. "That's difficult, sweetheart. I still don't know where she is."

Kathra hung her head. A whimper escaped her.

"But don't worry." Celeste placed a hand on hers. "Once I find out where she is, I'll take you to her."

"You'll be able to keep your promise sooner rather than later." J.R. stepped out of the bathroom shadows.

Celeste swung around. "Who are you?"

"Doesn't matter." J.R. stepped closer, making Celeste back away. "What matters is who you are." He lifted a scanner of his own. On it was Celeste's employee profile. "Celeste Sinceré. Level 5 access, huh? Low, but enough to help us get Xena."

Celeste's eyes widened. "You're trying to steal Max's Silver Fox!"

Kathra exchanged a glance with J.R. She had no clue what Celeste was talking about.

"I won't help you." Celeste pressed herself against the wall. "I don't even know where she is."

"That's fine." J.R. grabbed her wrist, causing her hand to spread. "I just need this."

"Let me go!" Celeste writhed in his grasp.

"Shhh." J.R. pressed closer to her. "Be quiet. Kathra." He looked over his shoulder at her. "Get your stuff while I convince Celeste to help us."

Kathra dove under her bed where she had stashed her purse. She pulled on her shoes and grabbed her scanner. By the time she was ready, Celeste had calmed. Her ears were flat, and her eyes raged with fury, but she didn't move or shout anymore.

"Celeste has graciously decided to help us." J.R. held his mouth close to her ear. "Isn't that right?"

Celeste spat a curse at him.

"Not in front of the kid." J.R. pressed something against Celeste's lower back. Kathra couldn't see what it was, but she thought she saw a metallic gleam . . . a pole or . . . knife? Kathra decided not to try and figure it out.

"We'll have to sneak passed all those nurses." J.R. clicked his tongue. "This is not going to be easy. Keep close, Kat." He headed to the door.

"Wait, Mr. J.R. We can go out the window." Kathra unlocked the window. "See? There's a door back inside over there!"

J.R. maneuvered Celeste to the window and examined Kathra's escape route. "Nice, Kat. Okay, you first."

Kathra checked her scanner to make sure the guards were on their rounds on the other side of the building before she slipped out. She was one floor up, but it wasn't too bad a drop. She'd jumped out of trees this high before.

Celeste jumped next. As soon as she landed, she darted away. "Help! He—"

J.R. landed and snatched her arm. He hissed something in her ear. She quieted.

But the damage had been done. Voices rang out in the air. "Did you hear that?"

"Over there!"

"Grab my tail, Kat." J.R. waved his tail in her direction. "Hold on and don't let go." As soon as Kathra's hand closed around his tail, J.R. darted into the shadows—almost too fast for Kathra to keep up. He clasped his hand around Celeste's mouth and peered into the darkness.

Two guards appeared with their flashlights and guns drawn. They shone them around. The light bounced off the leaves, but J.R. remained absolutely still. With his dark fur and clothes and Celeste's gray fur, they blended into the shadows. Kathra tucked herself behind them and further into the leaves. Her white fur could give them away.

"I don't see anything," one guard said.

"False alarm."

"Better have them look through the video footage to be sure."

"I'll call it in."

Both the guards went back to their rounds, one of them talking into a walkie on his shoulder.

J.R. grinned. "Those camera codes Sherd gave came in handy," he muttered. "They won't find anything."

"Idiots," Celeste whispered, but she didn't dare shout again.

"Let's go." J.R. headed off, sticking to the shadows. "Hang tight, Kat."

Kathra gripped his tail tighter.

"Hey." J.R. looked at her over his shoulder. "Good thinking with the window. Smart girl."

Kathra beamed with pride.

CHAPTER 45

Celeste dragged her feet as that nasty crook pushed her down the empty hall. She had tried everything short of screaming to get away from this wolf Kathra called J.R. She dragged her feet; she squirmed; she tried to catch the eyes of people who walked passed. But J.R.'s arm was an inexorable bulk of muscle. She couldn't fight him. And she wasn't even sure if J.R. was aware she had been trying. As for the people they passed, Kathra always alerted him they were coming with that blasted scanner of hers. Before they'd see them, J.R. would shrink into the shadows to avoid them. And it was easy at this time of night, when the workday was done for most everyone. She could have screamed for help, but J.R. had a knife at her back. She doubted it was for show. So on she went, step by step, getting closer to the laboratories and betraying Max's trust. She had to think of something. She had to stop them!

"In there, Mr. J.R." Kathra stopped in front of the arched "MFP Research Laboratories" sign. "The signal's getting stronger and stronger."

"No. No, you can't make me!" Celeste pulled against J.R.'s grasp.

J.R. gripped her arm hard. "Shut up!" He pulled her to the door and pressed her hand against the handprint scanner. The door whooshed open. He pushed her inside, through the ultraviolet sterilizer, and toward another door.

"No." Celeste tried to pin her hands to her sides, but J.R. pulled her arm up and pressed her hand against the other handprint scanner. Warm, red light ran over them.

"Unauthorized personnel detected," the computer said.

"Hm." Celeste smirked at him. "Try to get through this."

Keeping hold of her, J.R. pulled a card from his belt and plugged it into one of the scanner's ports.

"Adding unauthorized users to guest list," the computer said. "Verbal User Access ID required to complete this action."

J.R. glared at her. "Well?"

Celeste bit her lips together. She wouldn't say a word.

"Look, I ain't messing around anymore." J.R. pulled Celeste's back to his chest and laid the knife's blade at her throat. She felt it shave some of her fur off.

Kathra gasped.

"Say it." He snarled in Celeste's ear.

Until this moment, Celeste hadn't thought he'd kill her in front of Kathra. Now she knew better. "User Access ID: R397287."

"Unauthorized Personnel is identified as two Guest Users," the computer said. "One time access granted."

"That's what I thought." J.R. pushed Celeste into the laboratory. A slit of light silhouetted the lab's furnishings and glinted off the glass beakers and test tubes. It was empty. Celeste hoped it would be filled with scientists, but everyone had left for the day.

"Kat, find the lights," J.R. said.

Celeste heard Kathra patter to the wall. The lights snapped on, making Celeste squint.

J.R. glanced around at the equipment and lab. His ears swiveled. "She ain't here." He rumbled deep in his throat before turning on Celeste. "Where is she?" He shook her hard.

"I don't know." Celeste shrunk away from him. "Max didn't tell me where he keeps her at night."

"You know, I don't believe you." J.R. bared all his teeth at her. His fur rose until he looked twice his size.

Celeste's knees gave way. She fell to the floor as J.R.'s massive frame consumed her vision. "Please . . . please don't hurt me."

"She's over there, Mr. J.R." Kathra pointed across the lab.

"Huh?" J.R. looked around the room. His fur instantly fell. "There's nothing there, Kat."

"But my scanner says so." Kathra took a moment to examine the screen. "She's there." She trotted over to a wall with equipment mounted on it. "Behind this wall."

"A secret room." J.R. flung Celeste away from him as if she were trash. She rolled to halt and tried to keep herself from bursting into tears.

J.R. ran his hands against the wall until he found something. He slid aside a section of the wall to reveal a handprint scanner. Immediately, he pulled his card from his belt.

Celeste clenched her teeth. She had to do something. She couldn't let J.R. walk about of here with Max's Silver Fox. But what could she do? She glanced around for inspiration. The red paint of the fire alarm caught her attention. Of course! If she tripped the alarm, Max would have to come down to evacuate the Silver Fox. It was her only chance.

Slowly . . . quietly . . . Celeste got to her feet as the door unlocked with a click. J.R. pulled it open. Through the gap between him and the door, Celeste caught sight of the Silver Fox sitting on a bed with her back to the door. In her hands was a sphere shedding a flickering, golden glow on the surroundings. She had one hand turned upward to hold it in place and was spinning it with her other hand. The strange thing was she didn't seem to be touching it at all.

The sight made Celeste pause in her trek to the fire alarm. It was a ball of pure electricity.

"Kid?" J.R. swung the door open. His booming voice jerked Celeste back to the task at hand. She kept watching them as she resumed her journey to the fire alarm.

The glowing sphere disappeared from the Silver Fox's hands. She swung around. "Mr. J.R.!" She vaulted over the bed into his arms. "I knew you'd come for me!"

Celeste didn't have much time before J.R. would be ready to leave. If she didn't act now, she'd be too late to stop him. She bolted to the wall and yanked the alarm. A shrill bell pierced the silence, clattering in her eardrums.

J.R. swung around.

"Now you'll never get out of here!" Celeste smiled in triumph. It faded when she saw J.R. charge toward her. She squeaked and dove out of his way.

He didn't chase after her. "Come on! Let's go!"

Kathra darted after him. The Silver Fox tried, but she collapsed halfway across the room. She screeched in pain.

"Kid?" J.R. darted back to her. "What's wrong?"

"They injected . . . I . . ." The Silver Fox held herself. "My muscles hurt every time I move too much."

"They injected . . ." J.R. turned his puzzled glare to Celeste. "What did you do?"

"Even if I knew I wouldn't tell you," Celeste said from her place against the wall. "I don't care what you do to me anymore. As long as Max gets you afterwards."

"Let's not get overly dramatic, Celeste." Max stepped into the lab beside her.

"Max!" Celeste jumped to her feet. "How'd you get here so fast?"

Max gave her a look. "The computer always notifies me when someone accesses this lab."

Celeste shrunk down. He knew she had betrayed his trust.

Without another word, he walked to the alarm, flipped it off, and picked up the phone mounted on the wall. He dialed some numbers. "Ladies and gentlemen, that was a false alarm, please disregard. False alarm; I repeat, false alarm." The words echoed from the intercom system overhead.

"There you are, you bastard!" J.R. growled, the corner of his lip quivering.

"When I received word Terrance Claybourne had hired some muscle to steal my intellectual property, I should have known you'd be along eventually." Max strode over to J.R. without any fear at all. "I have one question, though." Max cocked his head. "How'd Terrance find out about her?"

"This has nothing to do with Terrance Claybourne." J.R.'s ears were flat against his skull.

"Then what are you—" Max's phone beeped—a long high pitched tone. The emergency signal. "Hang on, J.R." And to Celeste's surprise, J.R. did. He waited until Max answered the phone, though he did take the time to check on the Silver Fox.

"Max, there's a break in at the R and D Department." Jordan yelled so loud Celeste heard him over the phone.

"What?" Max's ears flattened. "Stop them! Now!"

"That would be Vix liberating some of your top secret items for Terrance." J.R. stood again.

"If she's working for Terrance . . ." Max turned to J.R. "What are you doing here?"

"I should be the one asking the questions." J.R.'s fur rose. "What were you thinking? I let you come into my town and you pay me back by burning my buildings, shooting my friends, and stealing my kids?"

"Your kids?" Max's ears flicked back. "Oh, wait . . . it was you! You're the one who took her from Jelu before I got there. I did get reports you'd been hanging out there before the disaster. Did someone hire you? If so, why didn't you turn her over?"

J.R. snarled at him, all teeth bared. "None of your business. What is your business is what you did to what's mine!"

"Right." Max held his hands together. "Look, J.R. I'm sorry. I didn't know it was your town. I thought it was some random place you chose. I wouldn't have done it if I had known. I'm not stupid."

J.R.'s fur settled a bit. "Still . . . I can't let you off without teaching you a lesson, Max. And what are you thinking, injecting my Kid with stuff?"

"See, now we have a problem." Max picked something off one of the tables. It looked like a blood pressure sleeve. "You seem to have some sort of claim on her, and so do I. And unfortunately, I can't let you leave with her." He strapped it on his arm. "I'm not done with her yet."

Xena whimpered. She ducked behind J.R.

"Max, what are you doing?" Celeste's eyes widened. "You—you can't take him on!"

"Listen to her, Li'l Max." J.R. scoffed. "You're going to get yourself into a world of hurt."

"You'd be surprised how quickly the tables will turn, J.R." Max flexed the arm with the sleeve on it. "But don't worry. I won't hurt you too badly."

J.R. snarled. He lunged himself at Max.

Max stood still, a small smirk on his face. He didn't even flinch at the mass of fangs and muscle barreling toward him. Rather, he stood motionless, like a tall tower in the middle of a storm. Nothing could move him.

At that moment, Celeste knew she would follow him anywhere.

CHAPTER 46

J.R. rushed at Max, all his rage propelling him forward. Max was going to pay—for Melody, for Mr. Withers, for Kathra, and for Xena. J.R. drew his fist back to deliver a blow that would knock Max out and break his nose . . . at least. But—

Something was off. Max didn't move; didn't even flinch. He stood waiting for J.R. to come at him. He was up to something. But what?

Instinct told J.R. to think twice so he pulled his punch at the last minute, though his momentum carried him forward.

The air around Max seemed to condense into a clear, gelatin-like substance. It absorbed J.R.'s blow and then . . .

A force exploded from the air around Max and flung J.R. across the room. He crashed through bottles and beakers before slamming into the wall.

"Daddy!" Xena rushed toward J.R.

J.R. groaned, rubbing his head. "What the—"

"Surprised?" Max held the arm with the sleeve on it into the air. "It's something I've been working on . . . with this young lady's help, of course. This prototype provides me with an energy shield powered by bioelectricity."

J.R.'s eyes widened. "You figured it out!"

"I did. I created a mesh made of a special proprietary alloy I developed that amplifies electricity—like a Silver Fox's fur." Max grinned at Xena. "I couldn't have done it without you, sweetheart. It's why I can't let you leave."

Xena clutched J.R.'s sleeve. He could almost feel her fear as an electrical charge in the air.

"Back up, Kid." J.R. pulled himself to his feet. "I'll take care of this."

Max rolled his eyes. "Don't you know when you're outclassed, J.R.? I haven't even begun to develop the abilities of this prototype. All the powers of the Silver Foxes will be mine to wield!"

"Silver Foxes? What are you talking about?" J.R. said. "You've gone crazy, Max."

Max sighed. "I don't expect you to understand. But if you leave the girl, I'll let you go. You can even take the white kit with you. I have no use for her."

"No."

"What's the big deal? Is someone paying you to retrieve her? I'll match the price. I'll even exceed it for all the trouble I put you through. Name the figure."

"This ain't about money."

"True. Money never meant much to you." Max screwed his mouth into a thoughtful pout. "What are you doing with them anyway? This isn't you. This isn't your style. I can't imagine you giving up your life for these two brats."

J.R. glanced at the Xena and Kathra. They were counting on him to get them out of here and back home where it was safe. And Melody was counting on him to bring them home. He got into a fighter's crouch. "Get ready, Max. I'm coming for you."

"If you insist." Max shrugged. "But remember, you asked for it."

This time J.R. and Max rushed at each other. J.R. aimed another punch at Max's face, but Max jumped over him and landed behind him. J.R. swung around. Right! Max was like Xena—not powerful, but lithe and quick. He had to adjust. J.R. swiveled and turned, ducked under a blast Max had thrown, and grabbed Max's leg. He swung the fox around and hurled him across the room.

Max sailed through the air, twisting around as he went. He held out his arms and . . . and slowed down as he approached the wall. He bounced off and landed next to Celeste. "Take cover, Celeste," he said, his eyes never leaving J.R. "I don't want you getting hurt."

Celeste gazed at him a moment before retreating to the lab entrance's doorway.

J.R. didn't need to tell Xena and Kathra what to do. They had already ducked into the secret room where they watched through a sliver of open doorway.

Max rushed at J.R., swiping his arm in front of him as he came. J.R. saw the air rush before him—a rippling, hazy space in front of the energy blast. J.R. dodged it, but Max came right behind with a kick to the chest. Pain exploded in J.R.'s sternum. He staggered back. Max's kick was twice as powerful as it should be. Before J.R. could recover, Max punched J.R. over and over in his chest, stomach, and face. J.R. collapsed to the ground.

Max leapt into the air and bent his knee—a blow that could snap J.R.'s ribs. J.R. rolled out of the way and into a standing position. Spinning around he kicked Max in the stomach and followed it up with a punch to the face that threw Max into the far wall.

Finally, the upper hand. J.R. charged at Max with all his might. At the last moment, Max held up his hands to block J.R.'s attack. Drawing energy from this prototype, he threw a blast into J.R.'s face, slamming him into the ground. J.R. groaned. This couldn't be it. He had to get up. For Xena's sake.

A foot slammed into J.R.'s chest. Max stood over him. "It's amazing how this device increases my abilities." He examined the device on his arm. "Tess will be pleased with this field test. So . . ." He leaned in close to J.R.'s nose. "Now, how are we going to solve this little problem of ours? Will you leave her to me? Even now I'll pay you handsomely for the trouble you went through in coming here."

J.R.'s chest heaved up and down. "Never!"

"Too bad." Max raised his hands, and the energy built up in them.

"No!" Xena rushed out of the room. She plowed into Max. "Leave him alone!"

"Kid, get out of here!" J.R. said.

"Move!" Max shoved Xena aside.

She latched onto his arm. "Get off of him!" She pulled at Max so hard, her cheeks turned pink. "Leave my daddy alone!"

"That's it!" Max stepped off of J.R. to turn to Xena. He grabbed her shoulder. "You need to learn your place!" He raised his hand at her.

"Eep!" Xena flinched.

"Kid!" J.R. jumped to his feet. "Don't touch—" He froze mid-sentence.

Max's eyes had widened. He twitched and convulsed, but no sound came out of his mouth. All his fur stood on end. J.R. caught a waft of burning fur. Sparks flew.

"Mr. J.R.! Help!" Xena pulled and pulled away from Max. "I—I can't get him off!"

"What the—?" J.R. took a step forward.

"Oh, no! Oh, no! Oh, no!" Celeste darted over to them. "Get her off of him. Make her stop!"

"What's going on?"

Celeste clutched her hair. "She's electrocuting him! She's killing him!"

"Electri—wha?"

"Daddy . . ." Xena turned to him with tears pooling in her ears. "Help . . ."

"Do something!" Kathra shook his arm.

"I . . . I . . ." J.R. gaped at Xena tugging and Max twitching. His mind's gears screeched to a halt. For the first time in his life, J.R. had no idea what to do.

"Max, no! I won't let you do this!" Celeste scrambled for a pair of black, rubber insulated gloves hanging on the wall. She pulled them on, stepped into matching black rubber boots, then grabbed Max and pulled.

"Right." J.R.'s mind started to turn again. Donning a similar pair of rubber gloves and boots, he pried Max's fingers off of Xena's shoulders. Max fell to the floor with a thud.

Xena fell into J.R. and buried her face in his shirt. "Daddy . . ."

"It's okay, Kid." J.R. held her. "I got ya."

"You killed him!" Celeste dropped to Max's side. "You killed him, you little freak!"

"N-no!" Xena clutched J.R.'s shirt. "I-I didn't mean to!"

"Maybe we can revive him." Kathra held her scanner close to her chest. "But I don't know CPR."

Celeste gasped. She pried open Max's mouth, tilted his head backwards, pinched his nose, took a deep breath, and blew into his mouth. She breathed into him two times, then found his sternum and thrust down on it with the heel of her hands. She thrust down fifteen times and then breathed again.

"Come on, Max," she said as she pushed down on his chest. "Don't go! Please don't leave me alone!" She leaned over him again. Max gasped and coughed. His eyes snapped open.

"Max!" Celeste threw her arms around him. "You're okay . . ."

Max heaved and wheezed. He seemed to have trouble getting his breath.

"I'll get help!" Celeste dashed to the intercom. "I need medical personnel and security officers in Laboratory 2A immediately!"

"That's our cue to go." J.R. grabbed Xena's and Kathra's hands.

"Not so fast!" Celeste grabbed Max's gun out of his holster. "Don't move." She pointed it at them, gun shaking in her hands.

J.R. froze. He knew the type. The girl had been easily subdued when she had no one but herself to worry about. But with Max hurt, it wouldn't take much to make her to snap. To get out of this, he'd have to disarm her—literally and figuratively.

"Calm down, now." He let go of his girls' hands and raised his own in the air. He took a step toward her.

"Stay back!" Celeste clenched her teeth. "Get away from him!"

"You've never even held a gun before, have you?" J.R. stepped closer. "This isn't what you want. You don't want to shoot somebody."

"Oh, yeah?" Celeste fired. Her shot went wide, completely missing J.R.

A scream tore out of Xena. She fell to the ground, clutching her shoulder.

Celeste stepped back, her eyes wide. But she set her teeth and pointed the gun again. "I won't miss again."

J.R.'s lips retreated from his teeth. No more Mr. Nice Guy. He snatched the gun from her grasp and raised it to smack her over the head with it. Celeste squealed and covered her head. It would be so easy to shoot her and put her out of her misery . . .

But no! He had to get Xena and Kathra out before security showed up. Besides, he didn't want to do it in front of the girls. Instead he tossed the gun aside, scooped up Xena, and let Kathra grab his tail again. With a glare at Max's delirious face, he charged out of the lab.

Security was already converging on the area when J.R. tore down the hall. Half of them stormed after him while the other half poured into the lab.

"There you are!" Vix appeared beside him as he darted down the hall. "I ran into some trouble in the research department."

"I know. You set off security."

"So did you." Vix glanced behind her. "Though, thanks to that, I was able to get my tail out of my mess. You were the distraction I needed.

"Wasn't intentional."

"They're catching up." Vix stopped long enough to scoop Kathra in her arms. "Let's get moving." She darted faster down the hall.

"Thanks," J.R. motioned to Kathra as he kept up with her.

"It's not like you were going to leave them behind," Vix said.

"Mr. J.R., look!" Kathra held her scanner's screen out to him. "There's a door over there where there are no guards."

"Guess the brats come in handy after all." Vix rounded a corner in the direction Kathra had indicated. "Keep it up, kid."

J.R. charged after her, glad to have both his girls back. Under normal circumstances, he would have stopped to teach everyone in the complex a lesson—burn it to the ground like Max had his town. But revenge wasn't his priority this time—not with Xena and Kathra in his care. He had to get them far away from this place. He had to get them home.

CHAPTER 47

"I think we lost them," Vix said, peering around a tree.

She, J.R., and his girls had escaped out of the complex, thanks to Kathra's directions. Once out, they plunged into in the woods where they slipped into the shadows and hid themselves behind the trees. They waited until the security officers passed before making their way back to where they had left their speeders.

"You okay, Kid?" J.R. set Xena at the base of an elm tree. The moonlight filtered through the canopy and sparkled on Xena's fur. It was shinier than J.R. remembered. Max had called her a Silver Fo—no! J.R. shoved those thoughts aside and concentrated on his Kid. She needed him.

Vix flipped on a small, electric light that shed a soft, blue glow on the surroundings.

Xena sat under the shadow of the tree. She still clutched her shoulder, but made no other noise or movement.

"Let me see your shoulder." He took her arm in his hands.

Xena let go of it, allowing him to examine the wound. A hole bored into her shoulder. No blood, though. At the power level Celeste had it on, the laser must have cauterized the wound.

"It's deep," Kathra said, peering over his shoulder.

J.R. glanced at her. "Maybe you should stay over there, Kitten. I don't think you should be seeing this."

"Yikes!" Vix inhaled through her teeth. "I shouldn't be seeing it!"

"It's not that bad." Kathra kneeled close to Xena to better examine the shot. "I've already scanned it, and there are no infections. But we need to clean it out. Do we have some water and a clean cloth?"

Vix handed J.R. the light and retreated to her speeder. "I have alcohol wipes and cotton here."

"That's not going to work." Kathra shoved J.R. out of the way. "It's too deep for alcohol. I might need to give her stitches. Never done it before, but I've read all about it."

"Aren't you too young to be a doctor?" Vix put her hands on her hips. "Practicing without a license is illegal, you know. They put little girls in jail for that."

J.R. sighed. He didn't need Vix's attitude. Not now. "Don't you have anything we can use, Vix?"

"Let me see." Vix rummaged through her supplies. "Will this work?" She dug out a bottle of water and a bandana.

"It'll be perfect until we can get proper bandages on her." Kathra snatched it from Vix's hands. "Thanks."

"No problem. How did the little brat get herself shot, anyway?"

"Never mind, Vix," J.R. said.

"Fine. Don't tell me anything." Vix went back to her speeder. "I'll just look over all the goodies I got."

"You scored, then?" J.R. watched Kathra wash out the wound.

"Mostly schematics." Vix pulled a disk from one of her pockets. "Security found me before I could get any of the prototypes. Ol' Max sure is into bioelectrical components."

J.R.'s ears pricked. "What?"

"I found plans for electrical shields, lightning generators, anti-gravity devices . . . even weird experiments he's conducting on fur." Vix chuckled. "It's like he's trying to turn himself into a Silver Fox."

"You don't say." J.R. walked over to her. "He did all that . . . because of his experiments."

"You were right when you said they keep all the good stuff in there," Vix said. "I can't wait until ol' Terry sees what I nabbed."

"Sorry, Vix." J.R. snatched the disk from her hand. "I'll need to keep this."

"No way!" Vix tried to snatch it back. "That's worth a lot of money to me!"

"There are more important things than money." J.R. stowed the disk in his pocket as he went back to Xena.

"Since when?" Vix shouted, then devolved into muttered curses.

J.R. approached as Kathra started to wrap the bandana around Xena's wound. "It's not bad, Kid." He sat beside Xena. "You'll probably have a scar, but that's it. And when your fur grows in, no one will even see it."

Xena studied the makeshift bandage. She didn't utter a sound.

"Look, Kid . . ." J.R. ran both hands over his ears. "You're going to have to tell me what Max did to you in there. I have to know how he made you . . . electrified. I got people who can help me reverse it."

"He didn't do anything to me," Xena said, barely above a whisper.

"What are you talking about?" Kathra tied a knot in the bandana. "You electrocuted that guy. I saw you!"

Xena fingered her dressing. "Can we go home now? Please?"

J.R. lifted her chin to face him. "We are not going anywhere until you tell us what went on in there."

Xena averted her eyes. Her mouth pinched shut.

"No matter what he did to you, you can tell me." J.R. tilted to see her face. "It's not your fault."

"He didn't do anything to me, okay?" Xena gazed at her hands. "He took blood from me and made me do some physicals, but that's it. Everything else was me! And I . . . I almost killed him!" She buried her face in her hands.

J.R. patted her back. "I don't know what he told you, but—"

"Daddy, don't you get it!" Xena shouted. "I'm a freak! He didn't make me this way. I was the one making the electricity short out back home. It happens when I get mad . . . or scared."

J.R. glanced at Kathra. Her mouth had dropped open. "Xena, be reasonable—"

"You want proof? Watch this!" Xena held her hand out. Her fingers tensed and shifted, and her other hand clenched into a fist. A glowing ball materialized in her open hand and grew until it was the size of a softball. "It's pure electricity. I've been hiding it because I didn't want you to . . . to . . . get rid of me. I didn't want you to stop loving me."

"That's why Max wanted my book!" Kathra grabbed J.R.'s sleeve. "He took my book on Silver Foxes, Mr. J.R.! That's why!"

"What are you all talking about?"

J.R. jerked his head around. Vix stood behind him, her hand raised to pick his pocket.

"Enough, you two." J.R. swung around to face Vix. "We can talk when we get home."

"Forget it, J.R. I can catch the hint." Vix moseyed back to her speeder. "Now I understand why you won't let me keep the loot, so I'll leave daddy to deal with his kiddies."

J.R. caught her speeder's handle before she could drive off. "Don't tell anyone about this."

"Who would believe me?" Vix shoved his hand off. She sped off without another word.

"I know you too well, Vix." J.R. stared after her. "When money's involved, you have no sense. Come on, you two. We better get home."

Xena held her wounded arm. "You want me to come home with you?"

"Why wouldn't I?"

"I thought you wouldn't want to bother with me anymore."

"Ah, get over yourself, Kid." J.R. waved her off. "Come on, Kat."

She was already on the speeder.

J.R. watched his Kid walk to the speeder. "By the way, Kid, is it me or have you been calling me 'Daddy'?"

Xena stiffened, and her ears flattened. "Have I? Oops. D-do you mind?"

"Nah. It's better than 'Mr. J.R.' anyway," J.R. mounted the speeder. Not much room for all over them. "I didn't bring the platform, so you're going to have to be a little uncomfortable."

"It's okay." Xena sat behind Kathra and stretched her arms around her sister to hold onto his waist. "I don't mind, Daddy."

"I want to call you 'Daddy' too." Kathra bounced on the speeder seat. "Can I?"

J.R. stifled a smile. "No one's stopping you." He started the speeder.

Xena leaned her head on his back. "I love you, Mr. J.R."

"You mean 'Daddy.' " Kathra said, also leaning her head against his back.

And that was the sweetest sensation J.R. had ever experienced.

CHAPTER 48

Max parted his eyes then closed them. After a turn and a groan, he opened them again. The bed he was laying in was not his. White sheets covered him, and the sun was being blocked out by heavy, white, canvas curtains. The walls in this room had been painted white, and the air had a clean, slightly plastic smell to it. "Sterile" would be the word he would use to describe it.

His head was propped on fluffy pillows. To his left was a table filled with flowers and cards and balloons with "get well soon" printed on them. To his right, Celeste was curled up in a chair with a bag sitting at its base. A jacket covered her, though her bare feet were exposed. Her breathing was light and even.

Max sat up and winced. Pain shot down both his hands and his legs, and something tugged at the inside of his arm. He lifted the covers and looked at himself. An IV was attached to the inside of his elbow, and his arms and legs were covered in bandages. On his chest were sensors monitoring his vitals.

With a soft murmur Celeste stirred. When she turned to him, her eyes widened. "Max, you're awake!"

"What happened to me?" Max cleared his throat. His voice was hoarse.

"Don't you remember?"

Max glared at her. "Would I ask if I did?"

"Sorry. . ." Celeste tucked the sheets around him.

"Well?"

"Max, I'm so sorry. I didn't mean to let that wolf into your lab. He forced me to. He did. He had a knife, and—"

"Celeste, don't worry about it." Max laid his head back on the pillows. "The minute I saw J.R., I put together what happened. J.R.'s an unstoppable force. He would have killed you if you didn't do what he said."

"If I had known this would happen—and that he would steal your Silver Fox—I would have let him stab me in the medical ward."

"I'm glad you didn't." Max rubbed his sore legs. "I'd rather have you alive. You're more useful to me than the Silver Fox was."

Celeste's ears stood up. "I-I am?"

Max threw the sheet off of him again. "Why are my legs sore?"

"The doctors say when you get electrocuted, the electricity has to travel through your body and exit somewhere. It exited through your legs, apparently."

"Electrocuted?" Max searched his mind. He had no memory of it.

"The Silver Fox did it." Celeste bared her teeth. "The next time I see her, I'll wring her neck myself." Her fingers curled as if she was choking the life out of her right then.

Max raised his eyebrows as he watched her. Celeste had a dark streak he hadn't known about. As he watched her, he had a vague impression of . . . of her mouth on his. Did she kiss him? But no, she said he had been electrocuted. Then she must have been reviving him . . . which meant . . .

"Celeste." He turned to her with wide eyes. "You . . . saved my life, didn't you?"

Celeste's ears stood straight up. She averted her eyes, lowered her ears, and nodded.

Max let his ears angle backward. "And are you regretting that decision?"

"Of course not! It's just . . ." Celeste lowered her head. "If it wasn't for me, you wouldn't have been in the situation."

"And if it wasn't for you, I wouldn't have known the Silver Fox was in that town. And I wouldn't have gotten my disk." Max patted her hand. "You're the best business decision I ever made, Celeste."

Celeste gazed at him. Her lips widened in a smile.

"I'm sure I have a ton of work to catch up on." Max laid his head back down on his pillow. "How long was I out?"

"About two weeks. The doctors had you under an induced coma thingamajig."

Max set his feet on the floor. "I've got to get back to work."

Celeste caught his arm. "You can't, Max. The doctors say you have to rest. They said they'd have to sedate you again if you don't."

"I'd like to see them try."

Celeste held him fast. "Max, stop! If you don't I will make you!"

Max nearly burst into laughter, but the look in her eyes stopped him cold. He had no doubt she'd find a way to subdue him. Probably drug him in his sleep. He snatched his arm away from her. "How do you expect this business to run if I'm in the hospital?"

"I've been taking care of things." Celeste rubbed the back of her neck. "Though, not very well, I'm afraid. Everything's a mess. Jordan constantly argues with me; Jané is constantly undermining me; and the two of them are always trying to force Tess to tell them what's going on in the laboratories. It's been a nightmare keeping everything running. That's why I wanted you to wake up. I've been here every night begging the doctors."

"Perhaps it's a good thing all this happened. I think everyone could do with some restructuring." Max set his teeth and yanked the IV out of his arm.

Celeste hopped to her feet. "Max, you can't—"

Max held up his hand to stop her. "I won't overexert myself. If you let me leave, I'll let you handle most of it while I heal. Deal?"

"Will they just let you get up and walk out?" Celeste said in a more mellow tone. She helped him on his feet.

"It doesn't matter because I am." Max felt a cold breeze brush against his tail. His hospital gown left his backside exposed. "Can you get me some clothes, Celeste?"

"Here." Celeste held up a bag at the base of her chair. "I was hoping they'd let you go today."

Max took the bag and headed to the bathroom. He had been right to trust her. She was already anticipating his every need. But there was one more thing to take care of. She deserved it, after all she'd done.

"By the way, Celeste." Max paused at the bathroom door.

"Yes, Max?"

"Do you want to know the combination to my vault?" Max gave her a knowing smile. "You know, the one where your Freedom papers are kept?"

CHAPTER 49

The moon rose on two fox kits huddled behind a wolf on a speeder traveling sixty miles per hour. The older kit, a Silver Fox, kept nodding off. She was holding onto the younger kit, a white fox, who was fast asleep. The wolf was trying to make it to the next town as soon as he could. He didn't want them to have to sleep on the ground for a fourth night in a row, and he certainly didn't want them to slip off of the speeder and onto the road.

J.R. hit the accelerator and brought his speeder up to seventy. He flew past the city limits' sign, leaving him only a few seconds to read, "You are now entering New Jelu: a city brought to you by the GFG Corporation." J.R. refused to give the tagline a second thought. All he wanted to do was to find a remote place where two growing kits could find a soft bed to sleep in for the night. He wouldn't dare go to his place in the heart of the city's underworld—not with his kids.

Xena picked up her head with a start. "Mr. J.R., where are we?"

"Jelu." J.R. had never told her this is where he found her sitting among ruins and holding her whimpering, hungry sister. He saw no reason to tell her now.

"When will we get home?"

"Tomorrow. Tonight, we're staying in a hotel."

Xena made no response, and J.R. glanced back to make sure she hadn't fallen asleep again.

"Daddy?" Xena said.

J.R. smiled to himself. He liked the way it sounded. "Yeah, Kid?"

"Do you think I'm a freak because I'm a Silver Fox?"

"You've been a Silver Fox since I found you," J.R. said. "Nothing's changed because now we know it."

"You and Max and maybe other people know it too." Xena stroked her sister's hair. "I'm beginning to think I'm the reason the town you found me in was destroyed."

"It had nothing to do with you."

"You really think so?"

J.R.'s ears pointed, and he looked at her. "Everyone thinks Silver Foxes are a myth. No one would have known what you were. You weren't the reason."

For a moment J.R. heard nothing but the engine, but he knew Xena was processing what he had said.

"You're lying, aren't you?"

"Through my teeth."

Xena leaned her head on his back. "Once the news gets out, people are going to start coming after me, aren't they?"

J.R. pulled over to the side of the road. "I will never let anything happen to you, Kid. I will always take care of you."

Xena threw her arms around him. "I'm so glad you found us, Daddy."

"I'm glad you found me too, Kid."

ABOUT THE AUTHOR

M.R. Anglin first wrote *Silver Foxes* over 13 years ago, but her skills has a writer has improved since the book was first released. She resisted the idea of revising it for a long time but finally succumbed. Now the story is where she wants it to be, and she may be able to put it to rest.

Comments and questions are welcome and encouraged, so contact her via e-mail (michiewriter@yahoo.com), through notes and comments on deviantart (michelay.deviantart.com), Facebook (facebook.com/authoranglin), and Twitter (@authoranglin). In addition, she is making a thorough attempt to update her blog every Friday on her website (http://lyeland.com).

BOOKS BY THE AUTHOR

Silver Foxes Series

1. Silver Foxes
2. Winds of Change
3. Prelude to War
4. Into Expermia
5. Interlude: A Series of Shorts
6. Celebrity Dish
7. Six Weeks (Coming 2018)

Other Books

1. Lucas, Guardian of Truth
2. Prince of the Sun, Princess of the Moon (Rulers of the Galaxy Book 1)

Anthologies

1. Gods with Fur (FurPlanet 2016)
2. Dogs of War Vol. 2: Aftermath (FurPlanet 2017)
3. Extinct (Wolfsinger 2017)